The D'lberville Bayou Murders

TIM CONLEY

"Fair winds & following seas"

DEDICATION

My wife, Carmela, has been telling me I need to write more murder mysteries and I finally took her advice to heart. Hence the series of mysteries that have spun off of The Pleistocene Pig – a novel that I ghostwrote with David Paffrath. I so much enjoyed the protagonist, Agent Benoit, that I decided to spin him off with his own storylines. I dedicate this book to my wife who likes the Gulf Coast.

CONTENTS

ACKNOWLEDGMENTS

I would like to acknowledge my wife, Carmela and son, James (JD) who have stuck with me all these years while I somewhat ignored them to pay attention to my craft. Thanks, guys!

1 CASE FILE #601

October 15, 2014

Charlotte Bradley had set in front of her makeup mirror for over an hour trying to make herself the most alluring female at the dance that was taking place later that night at Romeo's Delight. She was going in spite of her mother's pleas – or maybe because of them. At age 22 she felt liberated by the fact that her mother should not be telling her what was right and wrong anymore.

She felt that she should be a free woman since she had met and exceeded the age of maturity for most women in the South. But no, her mother had other ideas and definitely wouldn't approve of the place where she was going tonight or the company she was planning to keep. Tonight she was sneaking out.

The clock downstairs struck nine as she went down the back stairs of her mother's old antebellum mansion. It was almost too easy to rig things so her mother would think she was still upstairs in her room studying for her nursing exams. A friend would call after a little while and her answering machine would pick up in such a way that mother would think she had answered the call.

1

Meanwhile she would be several miles away – meeting James on the Boardwalk. Her Miata made very little noise as she eased out of the access road leading to Highway 49. Traffic was light and it didn't take but a couple minutes to turn into the parking area along the beach. James wasn't there so she decided to wait.

Finally she opened the fire red door of her car and slid her long shapely legs with their four inch heels across the leather of her seat and swished her short flared skirt as she surveyed the beachfront. A look at her Guici watch told her that James was way late. Her lower lip pouted as she released a deep sigh and wondered if she shouldn't just leave without him.

"He said to meet him at the Pavilion," she muttered as she searched the area once more and then decided to walk down to the pagoda shaped swimming area. Maybe he was hiding from her on the beach side. He always did like to keep her guessing.

Charlotte called his name as she walked through the Pavilion and then stood looking at the tide that was coming back in. No James. "That bastard better not have stood me up!" She turned to leave and suddenly noticed the three guys who were standing in the entrance – watching her closely.

A ball of fear launched itself in the pit of her stomach and she decided she couldn't escape back the way that she had come. She turned and stepped down onto the wooden planks that ran at the water's edge.

Disaster struck immediately. The heel of her bright red pumps slipped between one of the cracks and she was trapped – gravity took over as she fell forward – twisting her ankle in the process.

"Now ain't this a lovely sight?" Rico Jaurez Sanchez remarked for his two buddies to take a look. The sight from their point of view was excellent. Charlotte had fallen forward and her skirt was askew and pushed up as she tried to get her foot out of her shoe so she could get up.

Long legs encased in a fine weave stocking, attached by bright red and black suspenders were highlighted by the short white slip that matched the creamy white of her panty. The boys had a vision of full womanhood to gaze upon and took their time in assisting her.

"Where are our manners?" Rico asked as he knelt and pulled her shoe out of the crack. "Is anything broken, Miss?"

Charlotte shook her head. "I don't think so. Just help me up so I can meet my boyfriend."

Rico shook his head from side to side and continued to hold her ankle. He had her at a definite disadvantage where she couldn't get up with him holding her without revealing even more of herself than she was ready to.

"Now, we came down here to have us a good time, didn't we lads? Didn't count on something so lovely falling into our laps. No sense in wasting it – now is there?"

His buddies admitted as much to be true and Rico pulled her ankle to the side so her skirt rode up even more – revealing that the patch of white he had seen was just that – a white highlight on a pair of black satin panties. She was dressed to kill.

"Looks like someone was wanting to get lucky tonight. Boys, I don't see how we can refuse to give her what she wants." He reached over and grabbed her other ankle as she struggled against him. "I like the feisty ones," his breath was course and smelled of stale cigars as he pulled her closer.

Charlotte screamed but had to admit that there probably was no one around to hear her. Rico pulled her closer and his right hand was on her crotch before she even saw him move. His fingers slid under the leg band of her panty and his middle finger found the mark he was looking for.

"Gentlemen, this woman is fine! She already is wet and just inviting us to accommodate her snatch. Earl, get down here and hold her while I partake of a little of the fine cuisine of our fair city."

Earl did as he was told and Rico unzipped his pants. He pulled her black and white panty aside once more and inserted his rather large maleness into her sweetness. She gasped as his full size was accommodated by her – even though she knew she was being raped.

It was feeling good and she tried her best to block it out – to no avail. He was having his way with her body and she couldn't resist.

As her neck and face got redder and she was showing signs of being flush, Rico turned to his friends. "Look at this boys! We got us one of those women who enjoys being raped. She is turning the same color as Knoff's sister when we took her. I'll bet you she is about ready to pop. Are you ready to have your orgasm?"

Charlotte tried to refuse to answer but her body was already well on the way to telling the truth. She arched her back and the buttons stretched the fabric of her blouse. Her head moved from side to side and this time the scream was primal. She was in the middle of her orgasm when Rico pulled out and told Knoff to take his place.

Feeling cheated, Charlotte didn't have much time to wonder as Knoff put his huge phallus inside her. Rico had gotten her warmed up and now the big man was taking his pleasure. Her orgasm took up where it had left off and she came multiple times as he surged in and out of her.

Earl unbuttoned her blouse and played inside her black and white bra as Knoff finished. Then he took his turn and she had no choice but to come again from the friction of the use the men were putting her to. She felt his hot sperm explode into her womb and she screamed with enjoyment.

The guys finally let her get to her knees but Rico stepped forward again and forced her to open her mouth. "You bite me, bitch and I'll cut your pretty throat from ear to ear. Now give me the blow job you were saving for your boyfriend."

Charlotte didn't want to but complied and Rico was soon ejaculating into her mouth. She had to struggle to keep up with him but some of it dribbled out the side of her mouth and stained her bra. Rico took out his switchblade and stuck it into the middle of her creamy throat – severing the artery with a quick flick of his hand.

Her eyes widened in shock and pain before she lost all control of her body and slumped back on the boards to lie still.

"What should we do with the body, Boss?" Knoff inquired.

"Throw it into the tide. The salt water will wash away all the evidence and we have ourselves a new ride. He held up her purse and shook her keys. "Let's ride boys!"

2 CASE FILE #602

October 18, 2014

Tina Marie Comer had just turned 26. She felt some days like she was already an old woman. It was a struggle going into the office and facing people who only wanted to dodge their association with the law. Her job consisted of handing out checks to cover another person's bail bonds. Some of the dregs of society traipsed through her office. She was often glad there were bars between her and some of the filth.

Today was no exception. The persons who came in were not of the kind she wanted to associate with and they often lounged against the divider between them as if they were in charge of everything in their universe and not wards of the court.

One such was trying to get a look down the front of her blouse. Rico Jaurez Sanchez leaned against the counter and tried his best to impress her that he was more than just a goon. He had been picked up the week before driving in a stolen car. To make matters worse – the car belonged to a young lady who had been brutally murdered. The court had let him out on bail as he had no priors. Tina shuddered just looking at him.

"I have my own pad over on the bayou," he was saying as she tried desperately to tune him out. Maybe you and I could get it together and do the jitterbug sometime."

The frown on her face made him realize she didn't know what he was referring to. Jitterbugging wasn't something polite society girls did in the United States. Only in his frame of reference was dancing referred to in that manner. Rico cleared his throat and tried to explain but she got up and went into the back of the office without giving him the time of day.

She came back a few moments later with a receipt for him to sign and then handed him the check to take to his attorney. But her abrupt departure had pissed him off. He wanted a piece of her and wouldn't be denied. He stomped out of the bail bonds office and informed his friends that he had acquired a new target.

Thus began the surveillance of Tina Marie Comer. Rico and his boys kept her under observation for the full weekend, each taking turns with the tail as she drove down Route 49 to 11th street where she lived in one of the Bedford apartments. They watched her as she went out for supper at the Half Shell and then returned home via one of the small malls where she just browsed. She wasn't in the mood to buy anything – which was unusual for her.

She got back to Apartment 204 sometime around 9pm and that's when Rico decided to strike. As she put her key in the door he pushed her forcefully enough to shock the breath from her body. She couldn't scream as he pushed her into her foyer and kicked her in the stomach as she tried to get up from the floor.

"Listen to me, bitch! From now on you will pay attention when I'm trying to talk to you. No more of you ignoring me like you did today at the bond place. I am important! Probably the most important person in your fragile existence at the moment. You got that?"

She tried to speak but couldn't. Terror enveloped her completely as she realized who she was dealing with. The stale stench of cigar smoke permeated the room and she almost gagged as he got up close and personal by tugging her half erect using the front of her blouse.

The fabric tore as he dug his fingernails into the flimsy material and she was left slumped back on the floor with her black bra the only thing between them. She tried to cover up her breasts but he smacked her hand with his own and lowered himself down so he was sitting on her chest. She almost lost what little breath she had as she gazed in terror up into his face.

She was certain he was going to kill her. Rico left no uncertainty that he could do just that. She tried to scream but nothing would come out.

Rico reached behind him and fumbled with the hem of her skirt. It didn't take him long to reach her most private area and to impress her that he knew just exactly what he was doing to her. He grasped the crotch of her Victoria Secret panty and ripped it out. Rico had free access to her and took advantage to plumb her depths.

"This girl is ready to be fucked," Rico remarked to the other two guys who had entered the apartment behind them and were closing the door. She heard the lock click and then sighed a bit when Rico stood up. But her freedom was short lived as he stepped out of his pants and lowered himself down onto her again. Only this time his maleness was in close proximity with her female parts.

Rico rocked back and forth a couple times and then she felt something hard and hot enter her body. She couldn't help it when he began moving in earnest and her body began to respond to the heat of the moment. It had clearly been too long since she had had that kind of treatment and she was shocked that he was getting to her so quickly.

In spite of herself, Tina was responding to Rico's male member. The heat and friction were making it impossible for her to resist. She felt well on the way to crashing through that barrier that separated her from a most private moment – she came with a fierceness that impressed the man riding her.

"Boys, look how this one is coming in spite of being raped. Have you ever considered that most women want to be taken forcibly?"

He pulled out and gave way to Knoff and then Earl as they each took their turns. Then Rico made her take him again and dispatched her as dispassionately as the last girl. The men looked around the apartment and found little that they wanted. Then they left.

Tina Marie lay in a pool of her own blood and was found by the landlord a couple days later when one of the tenants complained there was an odor coming from her apartment.

3 CASE FILE #604

October 21, 2014

Mary Alice Daniels had just turned 19 on Saturday, October 11. Her mother had promised that she could move in with her boyfriend when she was twenty and Mary Alice could hardly wait. She was waiting for him to pick her up from her place of work and they were going to go out to eat at Bonefish – where the Bang Bang Shrimp and pesto were to die for.

Jeremy was late as usual and Mary Alice tried not to be fidgety but she hated it when he didn't arrive on time. One of the things that people always said about her was that she was punctual. Being on time was a matter of the heart from her perspective and she tried to never keep anyone waiting.

She straightened out the pleats in her skirt and looked out into the Barnes & Noble parking lot again. No Jeremy. Looking at her cell phone did no good. His was obviously off since he hadn't answered any of her calls. She was about ready to call a cab and say to hell with the boy.

Mary Alice tried her mother's work number again but no one picked up and the call went to the answering service. She went back in to the reception desk and rummaged around through one of the drawers until she came up with a list of cab companies. There was one that was circled in red and she called them.

It took twenty minutes for them to show up and she still had no idea where her boyfriend was. So she got in the taxi and gave the driver her address. He pulled out on Highway 49 and turned left toward the Air Force base. Her street was just before the exit to Interstate 10 and they arrived there in about ten minutes.

She paid the cabbie and got out. No attention was paid to what the cabbie did after she walked up to the front door. The path to the house was covered with Wisteria Vines where he late father had tried to make the vines adhere to a trellis he had put up years ago. She remembered how cool the shade always was in the hot summers as she would sit on a hidden bench and read her books. Fond memories.

Mary Alice was putting the key into the lock when she felt herself being pushed forcefully into the door. She tried to scream but a gloved hand was placed over her mouth.

"Scream and you're dead," a rough voice hissed in her ear as the assailant pressed himself against her. In spite of herself she felt his manhood pressing into her through their clothing and instantly knew she wasn't going to get away without giving something away. She was a virgin and good little Catholic girls didn't give that away easily. Her heart sank as she realized she might not be able to wear white on her wedding day.

Rico pressed her into the door as he turned the knob. He really liked the feel of control he got when his victims realized they were not strong to get away from him. He felt her body sag slightly and pushed her against an over-stuffed couch that was about six feet from the front door. He forcefully shoved her head down and began his task of violating her as his friends came into the house.

Mary Alice screamed as he entered her body. The pain was excruciating as her hymen broke and blood trickled down her legs. Rico didn't mind. It just made her a little slick as he slid in and out of her. When he figured he had broken her in good, he stepped aside and Knoff took over. Mary Alice really knew pain then as the big man was ever bit of a bull in a china shop. The other man turned out to be slightly smaller in that department but it was still not what she had desired for her first time.

Rico crowed as he surveyed the house, waiting on Earl to finish. "Boys, from the look of the bright red blood on the head of my dick, I would say we just deflowered a virgin. Now how about the odds of that. We pick up a virgin and have our way with her. Earl, are you about finished? I want me some more of that."

Earl grunted a couple times and then stepped back to allow Rico to have what he wanted. Her pussy had felt so good that he wanted to feel it again.

"Rico, you don't have to do it this time. I want her again."

"You had your chance, Ace. Now I'm going to get off on this one and we are going to go get us something to eat with the money Knoff is holding in his hot little hands."

They both looked across the room where Knoff was counting hundred dollar bills. "Geez, Rico. We ain't never come across a stash like this before. We need to start robbing houses."

Rico poked Mary Alice in the shoulder with his finger and asked what she needed with that much money.

"It's for my wedding dress, you moron," she gasped.

"Well, well. For a white dress you're only going to wear once and then hang in some closet. We are going to save you the trouble."

He pulled her up by her hair and licked her neck. She begged him to let her go, but he drew his switchblade across her throat and then started pumping like mad as she lost touch with reality. He finished and let her sag over the arm of the couch.

"Let's go eat, boys."

4 THE ASSIGNMENT

October 30, 2014

Ex-FBI agent Benoit hung up the phone and sat quietly for several moments, puzzled by the nature of the call. For sure, the caller had presented evidence that led him to believe his team could and should handle the assignment they had discussed. Talent was not the problem. And time also was not a factor. They had plenty of both and he had supreme confidence they could handle the assignment.

His problem wasn't logistics or timing, but the fact that the FBI would also be sending a team into the area to ramrod the affair of picking up the people who had already killed three girls in the vicinity of Biloxi, Mississippi. The Bureau would be thorough in their treatment of the case and would brook no trespass – especially from someone they now considered to be persona non grata.

After the Pleistocene issue had turned sour and ancient Entodonts rampaged the western USA for a couple months, Benoit and his team had been on the cutting block. Everything about the mission had been turned inside out – every order he had issued was called into question. Every person who lost their lives was laid at his feet. He was judged culpable and on several points – even negligent.

That aspect really didn't concern him. He had determined to turn in his badge and gun even before the assignment was over because of the way the Bureau had treated him in the field.

The second guessing and archaic methods of administration had gone straight up his nose. He had become upset with the way those higher up on the food chain had proposed to handle things once they got to the field. The fact that he and his team had already done a lot of the leg work was irrelevant to their plans. He felt he had known what was going on and was ready to close the door on the perps when his bosses moved in and changed or screwed up everything they had already done.

Ancient Entodonts had gotten loose because of the finger pointing and fumbling of the brass. People had died needlessly because they allowed some of the creatures to escape into the world. And that was after Benoit had everything buttoned up and was ready to shut the door on the ancient menace to society. But again, his orders were countermanded at the last moment and a marauding monster and its progeny had been unloosed on an unsuspecting public.

Benoit considered once more that they might not be welcome if they showed up in the area and began to nose around. They would need to go in under cover and remain under the radar for them to have any sort of effectiveness at all. And effectiveness in this case was to catch those responsible and bring them to justice. Not the sort of justice that included lawyers, court dates, judges and juries. Benoit was comfortable with the prospect that justice in this case was going to be swift and certain.

During his phone conversation the question had been asked if he had any problem whatsoever with accepting the fact that the person on the other end of the line wanted full control of the criminals and would not put them through the normal trial system that most Americans believed in. He had spoken the truth when he told her that he and his team were sick of the judicial system and wanted only to remove the filth from the streets – clearly different from his stance as an FBI agent.

After talking with the assembled members of his team, Benoit realized that every member thought the same.

They were ready to hand out some justice – especially after they viewed the photos that had been taken of the three girls. Brutal murders were no stranger to his team but he swore he had trouble looking dispassionately at the evidence and saw that his team was suffering from the same.

"We have to get these guys off the street," Desmond Howard muttered as they handed the pictures around. "These guys are animals and should be put down ASAP!"

Everyone murmured agreement. Benoit took the opportunity to broach the real power behind their assignment. "I'm here to tell you that we are going to be acting outside the law on this one. Our client wants for us to go in, snatch and grab – then turn over to her those responsible for her granddaughter's death. She wants no long arm of the law type of interference and has requested that I personally vet each one of my team to determine your stance on the acquisition and punishment of the targets. I will ask you now what you think and will take your word as bond. Anyone who wants out can sit the mission out here. No hard feelings or exclusions from future jobs because of your determination on this one.

Benoit looked around the room and asked each if they were IN or OUT. Unanimous. The steely look in the eyes of his team told him the whole truth. They would follow his lead through hell and gone.

He let out a sigh of relief and then continued. "Okay, we are going to have to go in under cover and remain covert the entire time. If we stick our heads up we'll get them chopped off. We have to get into the roles that we've designed for everyone and stay in them. The FBI can't know that we exist and will probably lock us up and throw away the key if they catch us. Anyone not comfortable with that?"

No one objected so Benoit turned the briefing over to his second in command and stepped back to observe the assignments. Russell Crowe stepped forward and began handing out folders.

"These have everything that has be gleaned so far. As stated, we go in covert and stay there. The Howards' will pack up and leave immediately. Melinda will become a third grade assistant at one of the local schools and Desmond will be trying to find manual labor of some sort. I've identified a chop shop that I think would make a good cover for him. The rest of you guys will go in as a biker gang. The local cops have to think we're just passing through, but the cover can be blown if we get made by the Bureau. They are going to be trying to tag all the players and unfortunately they will be paying attention to those who are just blowing through so be careful."

Benoit picked up the thread of the conversation. "The Howard family will find a place that we can all use as a refuge in time of storm. Otherwise, we stay away from them and allow them to be the upstanding citizens that they need to be. No one step out of line or bring attention to yourself and we should be able to pull this one off and get out of there. We leave tomorrow night at midnight, so get some rest and whatever you think you're going to need. Let's get these bastards."

Everyone uttered the sentiment and they all moved off to become engrossed in their own little worlds that would merge very quickly to become a force to be reckoned with. The GraveDiggers were on the prowl.

5 MILLING AROUND SMARTLY

Deputy Morgan Smith looked up from her desk by the big bay window and frowned. There was something eerie about the case files she had piled up on her desk. Sheriff Tackett had directed her before he went out on rounds to look for them for something that might tie in with the recent murders they had been having.

She had found two files in the three two-foot high stacks that could have any bearing whatsoever on the new cases. One of them detailed a murder of an elderly woman over in Pensacola who was stabbed in the throat. The other one had at least three involved in a murder/robbery and was west of Pensacola – up toward Foley, Alabama.

She glanced back down at the two files and re-read the exposition paragraphs again. There was no denying that she felt there might be something connecting them with the recent murders. Sheriff Tackett often remarked that tigers don't change their stripes and perpetrators don't change their method of operating (MO). If that were true then the murder in Pensacola might be connected to the ones in Biloxi.

She set the two folders aside and continued working through the piles. By the end of her shift she had six other folders – which she took in to the Sheriff's office to place in his IN basket. She then turned out her light and scooted out the door – ready for the weekend.

Deputy Smith wasn't too astonished when she walked in Monday morning to find the folders still in the Sheriff's basket – unopened and unread.

Tackett was in the bullpen area pasting stuff up on one of the three large boards they used to place their evidence for peer review. His normally red face was puffy and vibrant from the latest tirade he was indulging in.

"Listen, people. We need to get all the evidence up here on the boards that we have so the Feds, when they finally get here, will think that we've been on the job from the get-go." He saw Smith standing – looking at the boards, and directed some of his ire in her direction.

"Smith. What did you find on Friday that we can use to tie to these cases?"

"The folders are on your desk, sir. I found seven or eight close correlations between murders that happened over near and in Pensacola that might have bearing."

"Why wasn't I informed of this?"

Deputy Smith shrugged and continued looking at the photos that were attached to the boards. So the team had decided there was enough evidence to tie these three murders together.

"Smith! In my office! Now!"

Smith was startled by his directives and meekly followed him. He slammed the door and the next couple minutes were filled with surviving the tirade. Smith felt her cheeks get warmer as the vent continued. Tackett was going to have one of his fits someday and was not going to come down from it. This might be the day. Smith steeled herself for the threats to her job that were coming.

Sheriff Tackett finally took a deep breath and looked at the folders on his desk. He then realized that maybe his deputy had done her job after all and maybe he should have checked on his desk before he went off like a cyclone.

"I take it you think there might be a connection between these and the murders we have on our hands?" He weighed the folders in one hand and walked around to sit behind his desk. She took a deep breath and self-consciously wiped down the front of her uniform and stood in front of his desk.

"Yes, sir. I think two or three of them might be the work of the same people. Seems to be the same MO. And the perps in the Pensacola and Foley cases all indulged in gang rape and murder with a stiletto type blade. I think the connections are there."

Tackett looked down at the folders and then handed them across the desk for her to take. "Go through them and put the pertinent data up on the boards. Get it done quickly and let's get out there and see if we can find these guys. People are going to start freaking out if they think there are serial killers in our fair community."

Deputy Smith did as she was told and the department gathered around for a brain-storming session a couple hours later. Some of the staff wanted to go door to door but it was decided they didn't have the manpower for that – and that was something the FBI could do when they arrived. Several others talked about checking out the dives and clubs in the area. They all realized that leads to the killings weren't going to come easy. So they went to lunch.

6 EARLY MORNING PHONE CALL

The ringing of the phone interrupted Stanley Volgamore's breakfast. He hated that. People who normally called him knew he had certain times when he would accept calls. A full head of steam had built up by the time he lifted the receiver.

"Who is this and what do you want?"

The person on the other end of the line stammered – already at a disadvantage because of the belligerent tone of Lord Volgamore – whose friends were the only ones allowed to call him that.

"I was told you might be able to assist me with some things that my associates and I have picked up."

"Well, I can't. Don't bother calling me again. I ain't interested in anything you have to say. Good day."

Stanley started to hang up but decided to hear more. "What is it you are wanting to flog?"

Earl quickly got to the point. "We have stuff like TVs and a couple computers we need to sell at cost. We are trying to raise money for our great-aunt's surgery and would like to show some stuff to you. We understand you have an antique business and we would like to list some stuff through you. Is that alright?"

"Well, I don't appreciate having to take a call during my breakfast but you can bring some stuff, as you call it, by my shop this morning and I might be able to give some assistance. But I don't open up before 10 am. Be there after that and knock on the double doors at the back."

"Yes, sir. I will see you after 10. Thank you for entertaining us. We will make it worth your time, I assure you."

"I don't care about that. Just let me see what you have. Now good day sir. My bacon is getting cold."

Right after hanging up, Earl dialed another number. "We are on with old man Volgamore. He said to bring the stuff by after he opens at 10. Tell Rico that we need to move all the stuff on the first go around."

Earl hung up and began going through the stuff they had collected from several of the houses they had ransacked. There were laptop computers, desktop computers, fine china, silverware, quilts and other things that they had had presence of mind to take as they went through the old antebellum homes they had been invited into.

He was putting things into boxes when Rico called back. Rico didn't sound too enthused with the arrangement. "We can't be caught out on the street with too much or questions will be asked that we don't want to have to answer. So you only load one or two things and take pictures of the rest. If Volgamore can't be satisfied with that, then fuck him."

"Where am I going to get a camera at this time of morning?" His tone grated on Rico's nerves.

"Go to Walgreens and get a cheap one. They also have film developing there. Why do I have to do all the thinking for you? You and Knoff wear me out. I swear you are both idiots when it comes to thinking."

"That's why you are the Boss. You tell us what to do and how to make it happen and we do. I got to go if we are going to get everything done by his opening time."

"I don't give a fig about his opening time. The old man can get the stuff when we are ready to give it to him. If he is as shady as sources say he is – then we don't have to worry about him or his opening time. Just get it done. Got me?"

"Yes, Boss. Go ahead and send Knoff over with the van and we'll get it done."

They hung up and Rico threw his cell phone against the back of the over-stuffed couch – where it bounced off onto the hardwood floor. The back popped off and he reached down to put it back together. In doing so his eyes scanned the street outside and he zoned in on a fine looking girl who was walking her small dog.

The next half hour was spent finding out what house she had come out of. Rico's attention was glued to her legs. Long and very shapely under the wool skirt she was wearing to keep the chill of early morning away from her skin. Long blonde hair and a pretty face. He was convinced that she was his next girlfriend.

7 MISSION TO RIDE

Ronald Benoit, ex-FBI agent, finished packing his saddle bags and prepared to leave Kansas City for the Gulf Coast. He checked out his appearance once more in the full length mirror in his bedroom and decided he could pass for a biker.

His sideburns and scraggly beard had almost completely grown together and the dark wire-rimmed glasses set off his face with a look that said all he had to do was scowl and people would step out of his way. Leather vest over a black tee shirt topped his biker boots and he was complete.

Rose Morales, the team's physical evidence expert stepped into the room. She stood a short 5'5", was 115 lbs, blonde, blue eyes, 32 years old. Benoit knew she had 2 bullet wounds from a drive-by shooting when she was a teenager. She was his forensic expert for the team and was not afraid to do whatever it took to get the job done. She had follow Benoit and the team through hell and gone and had no love for organized crime or law enforcement following the PPG incident.

"Everyone is packed up and ready, Boss. How long do you estimate we'll be on the road?"

Benoit looked up sharply as he placed the last items in his saddle bag. "About two days if we take our time. We don't want to look like we're in a great hurry to get there. Probably wouldn't take more than eight hours if we barreled on through."

She stood in the door and looked for all the world like a typical biker chick. Skinny jeans, a Def Leopard tee shirt, red bandana around her forehead – tied in the back, and dark glasses. Her Nike boots had a stiletto sticking out of one side and Benoit knew there were other things tucked in nooks and crannies that would serve them well in a scrape.

"You've programmed the GPS to miss most of the speed traps on the way down," he suggested.

"Yes, we will skirt around most of the big cities on the way down and will probably only show on the radar once we hit the Gulf Coast. There's no way to get around all the traffic cameras once we get into Gulfport. They're all over the place. I'll find the best back entrances to the place after we get into the area."

"Sounds good, Rosie. Tell everyone to sync up their GPS with yours and let's get on the road. We have a mission to ride and I want to get this job over and done with as swiftly as we can. You know the FBI have been called in?"

"Yes, Desmond informed us. They won't give us a free ride if they discover who we are. Do you think they will detain any of us they come across?"

"No doubt about it. Remember what they told us in Great Falls. They don't want us messing around with anything regarding law enforcement. That's why we had to hire our doubles to make them think we are still in Kansas City. Don't want to set off their radar by knowing we aren't here anymore."

Rose walked over and looked out the window. The sun had gone down and there were no lights on in the courtyard. Most of the team had already mounted and were merely waiting for them to join the group.

She looked back at Benoit as he threw his saddle bags over his shoulder and strode toward the door.

"I think all of us are looking forward to this one ending well. And our benefactor's check sure helped make the mission start off with a good note."

"She was generous," Benoit admitted as they walked into the courtyard amid the startup of over a dozen Harleys. His voice was not to be heard over the rumble of so many bikes and he finished loading his and joined the procession as they moved out onto the road.

It was still light enough to see so they had turned off their headlamps. No sense in giving things away if someone were using overhead to monitor traffic in the area. Better to be cautious than sorry latter.

They spread out as the miles clicked by so that only two or three were riding together. Lights on and 90 mph – they were flying down the road in the dead of night – heading for the bayou – looking for a fight. Or at least looking for someone who needed to be brought to justice.

8 INFILTRATION THROUGH GULFPORT

Benoit let off the gas throttle and coasted to the side of the road. They had turned off Interstate 10 about an hour ago and now could see the lights along the strip leading into Gulfport. The team sat on their bikes as he pored over a plasticized map of the area.

He ran his finger down Route 49 and gave directions through his mike. "Desmond has already set up the primary safe house on Kelly Avenue. The address is 1730 Kelly. Sammy and Russell, you will go there and assist them. Melinda just texted to say for you guys to park around back of the house underneath the awning they set up this afternoon."

He paused for a moment and then continued. "Take Airport to Hewes Avenue. Hewes runs north and south all the way down to Railroad. Take it easy on the gas and try not to raise anyone's eyebrows. Turn west after you get on Railroad and Kelly is to the left after you pass the theme park on your right."

"Got it Boss. We'll meet you there." They pulled back out into light traffic and soon were out of sight. Benoit still could hear their Harleys as he gave his full attention to the rest of the group.

"The rest of us are going over to Owen Palmer park until in the morning. It's off of 3rd Street and within a mile or two of the safe house. Then once the sun comes up we will go on to the second safe house on Jones Avenue. Address is 1410 if we get split up. Again, park in the back."

He folded the map and placed it inside his biker's vest. "There is an old barn that is still standing on the property and we need to go in there one at a time. Say in half hour increments. Don't want to alert any overhead that a bunch of us are here. Just trickle in and they might not make any associations."

Everyone nodded and they too pulled back out into traffic. The sun would be up in a couple hours and they knew they had to take their time. It was obvious to everyone that the FBI had selected the area as a hot spot. All resources would be trained on the area along the beach to detect any suspicious movements in and out of the vicinity.

They pulled into the park and left their bikes under the trees. Benoit led them over to a Waffle House and they had a leisurely breakfast of bacon, eggs and grits. One by one they disappeared after the sun had come up. Benoit paid the bill for them and finally walked back over to the park.

He was sitting on his bike when Rose Morales sent him a text. They had to keep it short and in the clear since using a scrambled transmission would have certainly alerted anyone who was looking for that type of communication.

"Gators," was the key word they were using to communicate they had arrived safely and without notice. Benoit sent back his countersign of "Roger Rabbit" and shut down his phone to await the next transmission – which came about 45 minutes later. The same word was sent and acknowledged. Then Benoit rumbled out of the park – destination: the safe house on Jones Avenue.

He arrived about an hour later and pulled into the barn. He waited for about fifteen minutes before walking in the back door of their hiding place. Rose Morales met him with a cup of coffee.

"You almost waited too long. It's starting to get cold. I can warm it up for you, if you want."

"No, Rose. I can appreciate it better if it ain't so hot. Really appreciate it. Everyone else is ready?"

"Yes. We are all ready to rock and roll. Got any specific ideas of where to begin looking?"

Benoit walked down the stairs to the basement and Rose pulled the door closed before he said anything else.

"From now on we only speak when we are down here." He looked over the faces that looked up from their screens and maps. Make sure the cover keeps running upstairs."

"We got local TV taking care of that," Sammy remarked, looking up from the items he was placing on the action board. "We don't have to worry about that. And we just finished the tie in to the local leo's comms system. Anything they tell the FBI will be ours if they use their radios or computers. We will get a bug into their offices tonight."

"Roger that. Do we know if they've been swept for bugs?"

Russell nodded. "That is the first thing the Feds did when they arrived. They only beat us in by about twelve hours. Not enough time for them to completely get set up. But they searched for bugs. Probably won't do that again for a couple days. By then we should know everything they do and then we can detonate the little beasts and they won't know anything was there."

Benoit sat his coffee cup down and noticed it was empty. "We can't afford to take anything for granted on this one. If I know the FBI director, he won't leave any stone unturned. I'll bet they already have someone in their sights."

Everyone sat quietly for a few moments and then all heads turned to the speaker that had just activated. The screen indicated it was coming from the Sheriff's office.

"We have to appear to be helping the Feds. Don't give them anything until you make me aware of it first. We have to maintain our distance from them guys. Everyone got that?"

Sounds of assent could be heard. Benoit waited a moment. "Looks like they already have dissention in the camp. Well, let's get to work. I'm sure the Feds also heard that."

9 HANGING OUT IN BARS

Not much in the way of sleep developed during the night. The team of Grave Diggers was too tightly wound up for sleep to overtake them. The police chatter alerted everyone to the fact that there was more going on than met the eye. They all knew they would have to be vigilant if and when they went into the community.

Ronald Benoit slept fitfully for a couple hours and then accepted a cup of coffee from a pot that Rose had been nursing most of the night. It was foul, but woke him up. He was listening to the bug in the Sheriff's office when the rest of the team joined him around 6am.

"Sheriff Tackett has just instructed his men to go in and bust a biker gang down on 18th Street. Some place called the Fisherman's Tavern. Rosie, you and Clint ride over there once the police have left and see what the fall out is. We need to make friends with some of these owners so they can tip us off when they hear something going down."

"What are we looking for specifically?" asked Clint as he took his Glock out and checked the magazine.

"Anything we can use that might put us on the trail of our serial killers. Some low-life out there is going to enjoy spilling the beans on any action they think is going down. Especially if they think the police are involved in the active search."

Around 10am he gave the green light and Rosie climbed on the back of Clint's bike. Their trip to the tavern in question was along the back streets and they raised no alarm among the local law that would have alerted someone to another gang being in town.

Meanwhile, Benoit took a back route of his own and went over to the other safe house. Desmond met him at the door and they quickly got each other up to speed on the situation and their plans for the days ahead.

"Desmond, your team is going to be our brains in this city. You have the feeds from the bugs and can pass information on to the guys we put in the field. Let us know when any sort of law moves in our direction. I don't have to tell you we have to operate under the radar. And especially where the FBI is concerned."

"We understand. And we've already seen some mention from the Sheriff's band that the Feds believe there is an unwanted biker gang in the city, but they think we're already past Gulfport and moving into Pensacola."

"That's good news. Any idea who they are?"

"We think they might be the Silcox gang who were operating in Texas for a while. Not sure why they would have moved out of Dallas but the number of bikes and composition fits. Looks like they might nail down the Feds for us for a week or so."

Benoit nodded. "Let's hope we have our men by the time they get Silcox and his boys nailed down. What else you got?"

"Sheriff Tackett was just briefing his people on what to do if or when they do find out who the perps are. He also just authorized the use of deadly force."

Benoit rubbed his hand through his thinning hair and whistled. "Is he serious?"

"Sounded that way to me. Apparently the Feds briefed him early this morning regarding the use of force. We didn't get privy to that briefing but it appears they are serious about it."

Benoit tapped his headset. Everyone in the team listened up and received the following message – "D F" repeat "D F". All of them knew what it meant and went about their business with even more caution. They were one step away from being under a red flag where they would pack up and regroup in a pre-selected place.

"Rosie and Clint haven't reported in yet. Maybe that will cause them to let us know what is going on at the Fisherman's Tavern over on 18th and Railroad. I sent them over to gain some on the ground information. It should be coming to you soon. You guys are doing good work. Keep it up."

Meanwhile, Rosie had snuggled up against the owner of the tavern, a black Creole by the name of Jim Whiskey. Jim had an affection for biker babes – mainly because most of them had the morals of alley cats and no time to be wasting. Rosie seemed she was his type. She did nothing to cause him to think otherwise.

"What did the cops do in here this morning?" she inquired.

"How do you know the cops were here?"

She smiled sweetly and settled on the stool so he was standing between her legs. He reached down to stroke the seam of her jeans as she replied softly. "We were about to turn in here when we saw them arrive. Did the splits to make sure they didn't see us. So what were they after?"

"Don't know that they were after anything," he replied as he slid his hand underneath her halter top and tried to cop a feel. She moved around so he missed.

"Well, stud. Before I put my feet down anywhere I have to know that I'm not going to be nicked by the law. Number one rule with me and my mate over there in the corner. Now, he doesn't mind when another man feels me up, but he does mind when it happens that we get into a bind with the law. Nothing worse than to wake up with a riot shotgun in your face. So take my questions as my way of preserving my fair hide."

"I gotcha baby. They cleared out my bar and told me that I was to entertain no more bikers for a while. Seems they might be looking for someone who has killed some dames."

Rosie let his hands find their mark and giggled a bit as Jim Whiskey had his way with her. About an hour later she and Clint walked out the door and mounted their bike. She communicated with Desmond as they were motoring and the information was passed on to Benoit who had just visited another bar and received similar information.

'Looks like they're serious about putting a crimp on movement around here. Also about finding someone.' He thought to himself as he got in a rental car and drove back to their hideout.

10 A RUN-IN WITH THE FEDS

Benoit looked up from his beer at the Lady Slipper and froze in place. He had changed into jeans and a button down shirt – to fit in with the locals. The Lady Slipper had been named for an exotic dancer from the early 70's. She had gone missing after her last performance and the name just seemed to carry on without her.

Two Feds were followed by another two. They fanned out through the room checking credentials. Those having none were pushed through the door by the last team in. They made their way around the bar and finally stood at Benoit's table.

"Drinking alone, are we?" a six foot four long arm of the law addressed Ronald.

He nodded and tipped his bottle in their direction. "Just stopped in for a tall cool one before going home to the little lady. Not looking for trouble."

"Well, you just might find it. Let's see some kind of ID. Driver's license maybe. Social Security card. A picture of the little lady might help."

Benoit reached into his hip pocket and retrieved his wallet – which he tossed on the table. The Fed picked it up and rummaged through it – checking the address carefully.

"This says you live over on Highway 49. Which side of the tracks you live on?"

"Ain't no tracks go up 49. They run parallel. I live in a trailer park across from the 17th Street Seaworld Museum. It's closed now but my kids used to enjoy going in there."

"Is that so? Gainfully employed, are we?"

"Yep. Over on St. Johns – at the plastic factory. We make bags so everyone else can clean up their litter and leaves and such. Foreman's name is Randolf. Don't know his first name. People just call him Randolf."

"You have his phone number?"

"Nope. Never needed to call in. I just don't think it's right to take a paycheck from someone and not show up for work. Do you mind telling me what this third degree is all about?"

"No. We have orders to check out everyone. Keep your nose clean and we won't have to have this conversation again."

He threw Benoit's wallet back onto the table between them and walked away. Ronald was left with the feeling that the FBI had just scrutinized him to the fullest extent of their ability. They would find nothing – of that he was sure. Desmond had searched for just the right person and had found one that Ronald looked alike enough to fool most people.

He showed up at the plastics factory the next day for his shift and wasn't too surprised when the same FBI agents showed up – checking him and his cover story. Randolf showed them back to where Ronald was loading squashed bottles into a machine.

"Feel lucky you didn't waste our time by lying to us yesterday. Can't say the same for the rest of your Southern gentlemen. We've spent a ghastly morning trying to catch up with some of them. When is your shift over?"

"4:30 today. Most days we work until 6:30 but the evening shift ain't coming in today. Something about orders not moving too fast right now. Hope it picks up soon."

"You get laid off a lot here?" asked the second Fed – who was starting to sport a mustache. It was obvious from the way he rubbed at it with the back of his index finger.

Benoit heaved the tub of plastic into the machine and turned on the gears that would extrude it through the heating coils within. He stood back and looked at the Feds.

"What are you guys really looking for? I know you aren't wasting our tax dollars in rousting bars and hanging out with the working folks. So what gives?"

"Can't tell you that. Just a word of advice for one of the guys who is working. You probably need to just go home today and leave the drinking to someone else. We are conducting an intense investigation and want to know who all the players are. And we'll probably need to speak with your wife to verify your coming and going for the past couple days."

The second man leaned over and looked inside the hopper. "You don't know who could be out there on the streets now. Be safer for everyone just to stay in their homes. Now be a good boy and go home after work, huh?"

Benoit nodded and continued filling up another load as the Feds walked back toward the front of the factory. 'I'll for sure be a good boy,' he thought as he looked into the mouth of the machine and found the bug the rookie had placed there. 'For sure I will.'

11 WARNED OFF THE CASE

Russell Crowe turned his bike into the Piggly-Wiggly parking lot and sat for a moment just looking at the people going in and out of the establishment. Most of them – especially the young mothers, were skittish. Something other than buying groceries was on their minds.

Judging by what they had been seeing the last couple days on what WKBQ had termed the "Butcher Shop" killings, he wasn't too surprised. They had called it that because of the way the killers were dispatching their victims. Always with a knife to the throat – bleeding them out.

He went inside with the list Melinda had given him and grabbed a rickety-wheeled cart. He frowned and took it back to exchange it. A young woman was definitely showing signs of not trusting anyone as he offered her one that he had pulled out of line. It seemed the news media had really hit the nail with their advice to everyone – stay home, don't open your door, go out only if you have to.

He tried to concentrate on his list but things became sticky when he saw a couple teams of Feds come into the store and fan out. They worked the isles methodically and finally got to him as he was loading chickens in his cart.

"Is there some reason you're stocking up?" the lead FBI agent asked.

"Well, my wife sent me to get food for a cookout we're having this weekend." He held up his list and the agent took it. After looking at it he handed it back.

"And what is your wife's name?"

"Melinda. Melinda Crowe."

"She have a phone number?"

"Yes, she has."

"Well, we don't have all day. What is her number?"

"616-7219. It's a local number."

The agent dialed the number and asked for Melinda Crowe. She answered his questions and the agent seemed to relax a bit. He indicated to his second to move on to the next person.

Russell took a chance and inquired about what was going on. "The people around here seem to be afraid of something. What is going on?"

"I can't discuss an ongoing investigation with you. How long you lived down here?"

"About ten years now. Came down from Missouri after one of the bad floods they had up there. We both got good jobs and have stayed. The news was saying something last night about some girls being killed along Highway 49. Is that why you're stopping everyone?"

"We are just trying to make sure everyone is accounted for. Where are you going to have your cookout?"

Russell scuffed one boot over the other but answered. "We thought about going over to the park near D'lberville. It has a good picnic area and the kids like the water there. Kind of protected by the bayou there. Ever been over there?"

The agent shook his head. "Can't say that I have. When are you planning on going over there?"

"Sunday afternoon. You're welcome to come on over. You don't work all the time, do you? We all need to take some time off and enjoy ourselves. Hot dogs and beer go down good out there."

"I might just do that. Now you have a good day." He walked away and Russell was left with the feeling they had better follow up on the picnic idea. He called Benoit and Melinda to let them know about the interview. Benoit admitted that they might indeed have to follow up.

The next day that feeling came to fruition as Agent James showed up. He accepted a beer and some barbequed chicken and sat nervously for about a half hour. Then he looked directly at Melinda.

"Mrs. Crowe. Would you mind coming down to the FBI HQ with us? There are questions we need to ask you."

Russell left his seat on the tailgate of the old pickup and made his opinion known. Now, listen. You come into our camp and eat our food and then want my wife to go downtown. What are you playing at?"

"Sir, we've checked out Mrs. Crowe and didn't find any marriage certificate for her. We are just trying to find out who everyone down here is. It probably isn't anything but we have to punch every ticket to make sure everyone is who they say they are. Now can you explain why she doesn't have a marriage certificate?"

Russell thought fast. "Yes, I can. You see, we were married but never filed it with the local magistrate. In Missouri you have 60 days to file and we kind of forgot. But she is my wife. I can assure you of that."

Agent James looked from one to the other, then surprised everyone by asking one of the kids how long their mother had been married.

"Over ten years. I'm 12 and mother had me by some mean bastard before she married Dad. He has been good to us."

"All the same, I want you to come downtown tomorrow and do some fingerprints and background check for us. We have your address and won't hesitate to haul you in if you don't appear. For now enjoy your picnic and your family."

He set his beer down and walked over to his car. "I'm only doing my job. See you tomorrow."

Russell and Melinda's eyes met as the car disappeared. Neither said a word but quickly looked about the campsite for the bug they fully anticipated finding. It was attached to the bottom of the plate that Agent James had been using. It was so thin they would have discarded it with the trash when they packed up.

They left it and continued to have their picnic. Normal talk about normal things. Every now and then Russell vented about the FBI trying to intimidate them – that would have been expected.

12 THE FEDS SET UP ROADBLOCKS

Sammy Blackman and Clint Black left very early in the morning and attempted to go north from Keesler Air Force Base along Highway 110 but found the way was blocked by the FBI – who were searching vehicles and detaining those they considered to be suspicious. The men sat in gridlock for hours and finally got off on a side street and returned to their safe house – without going to Pensacola to check out a couple leads.

Benoit took it all in and came to the same conclusion they others had already entertained. The Feds were stepping up their search around the D'Iberville area.

"They think they have a lead of some sort," reported Desmond from his stool in front of the bank of listening devices. "They are also looking for our people out on route 49 coming into Gulfport. Melinda is a prime suspect now in their investigations since she didn't show up for the interview. How are we going to find what we're looking for if they keep this up?"

Benoit sat at the table they used for meals and nursed a strong cup of coffee for a few minutes. He was deep in thought as they others banged about various ideas. Finally he set his coffee down and they all looked in his direction.

"We continue to stay under their radar. We set back and listen in while they beat the bushes. Otherwise we get tangled up in their schemes like we almost did yesterday. We can't have that and we are certainly going to have to arrange something."

"What can we arrange that they won't be able to unravel in no time? Remember – they have a whole lot of high tech at their disposal. And they don't like to be messed with."

"Yes, I know. And that might just play to our advantage. We can throw a red herring into their midst and make them think they have something. Gather round and let's scheme and plot."

That night there was a break-in at several of the morgues. In two of them nothing was taken. In another a youngish woman was found on the slab when the medical examiners came in the next morning.

They thought she might have been laid out earlier and so began an extensive examination on her. She had been a burn victim from a car accident – so a good extent of her body was charred. The thing that hadn't been burned was her left hand. They were able to get fingerprints from it and promptly sent them off to the FBI headquarters in Biloxi to be analyzed and confirmed.

Several hours later they got confirmation that the ruse had worked. Desmond reported the Feds had made a positive ID and had determined she was from Missouri and was definitely their person of interest. It appeared she had been trying to evade having to appear. They labeled that part of their investigation closed.

"So what do we do now?" Rosie asked.

"We inform the Boss of what has developed. Then we go out and search for ourselves.

Rosie looked curiously at Desmond. "You think we can find something the Feds haven't? There are some killers out there and the Feds are just beating the bushes. How about the local cops? What are they doing?"

"Nothing. Absolutely nothing. In fact, they aren't even doing nightly patrols any more. This city could be looted and plundered and they wouldn't raise a fist. I think the Feds have them running scared. And the media isn't helping."

Rosie sat back and nodded her agreement.

Clint came into the room with his backpack. Desmond and Rosie both perked up.

"Going out somewhere, are we?" Desmond inquired.

"As a matter of fact, yeah. How do I look?" He turned on his heel and let them take in the tattered rags he was wearing. The Boss wants me to go and sit out on the boardwalk and take in the sun all day. Thinks I might be able to spot something. Or be spotted observing and give our friends in the law enforcement agencies something to focus on. Wish me luck."

They did and he disappeared. Clint was an expert tracker and also knew how to expertly hide – often in plain sight. He would drive the Feds crazy. Desmond shook his head and grinned.

"What are you grinning about?" Rosie asked.

"Leave it to the Boss to come up with some way of fucking with them stuffed-shirts. Clint will have the bastards chasing their tails for days. And we will get some much needed intelligence from them. I can hardly wait."

Rosie poured them both another cup of coffee and they both set back to wait. It certainly didn't take long before the FBI and the local Sheriff's office were buzzing with a new lead. Then they lost him and the search really began in earnest.

Benoit stopped in as they were listening to the law becoming more porous and spread out. "Sounds like we've unleashed a fine kettle of fish on them, huh?"

They all grinned and listened.

13 LEAVING THE SCENE

"The Feds are getting too close," Ronald Benoit told his team as they were considering their options at the morning meeting. "We don't know when they are going to start working this side of the tracks, but it will undoubtedly be too soon."

He glanced around the room and saw the stiffness in everyone's backs. They didn't want to have to pack up and go to a new residence. Clint said what was on their minds.

"It will take at least a week to pack up, find a place that has already been swept, set up again and get the intel flowing again. I say we remain, but take it all underground. You know we have the basement and Desmond and I are excellent carpenters. We can make it so they won't find a thing – ever. Not even a hint that there could be something else here."

Desmond nodded vigorously. He was as pissed as the rest of the group that they hadn't been able to make any headway in the investigations. His face showed his frustrations and all the rest were no closer to controlling their own emotions.

"Listen, Boss. We didn't come down here and take this job to run from the authorities."

Benoit held up his hands. "But that is exactly what you are going to do. You and Melinda and Clint are going to mount up and get out of Dodge. You're going to make enough noise in going to convince them that there is another angle to this game."

He didn't wait for protests that he knew were coming. "We will use the time that you guys are giving us to put this place under wraps. When you've shaken off the posse you can sneak back in and resume operations at full staff. But right now we need to make it appear that our troop has departed the area. Got it?"

Everyone nodded and Desmond hopped down off his stool. "How far do you want us to take them?"

Benoit thought for a moment. "Just to Southaven. Slip into Memphis and then go to ground. Make sure the Feds have a tail on you to that point and then just disappear. You can be back here before them. Odds are it will take several days before they figure out you are no longer around. We can use that time while their forces are diminished to make some headway."

Melinda joined her husband in packing their saddlebags and they left with Clint – in route to a trip to draw the Feds off their trail.

Their first trick was to knock over a convenience store on 13th Street – just off Railway. The call went into the Sheriff's office and was passed almost immediately on to the FBI. Six agents went screaming out of the area – in hot pursuit.

The fact that there were three of them – all presumably male, lit up the Fed's radar. Interstate 55 was crawling with the law by the time they made the state line. Their motorcycles were tagged and the law enforcement thought they were moving in for the kill – only to find out their quarry was nowhere to be found.

Their bikes were found. No fingerprints, DNA or anything of substance that could lead anyone to conclude they had evidence that might break the case open. The Feds were stymied. And calls into headquarters didn't do too much to settle their stomachs after they were told to dig deeper and not come back without every stone in Memphis having been turned over.

"The fact is our main suspects just went to ground in that town. They can't be allowed to escape. The main body of the FBI will be in Memphis tomorrow morning and we are going to tear that place apart. Just get started on containing everything going into and out of the place."

Benoit and his staff knew the moment the decision was made and wasted little time in springing into action. "The Feds are making a big mistake by pulling most of their people out of here. We should be able to locate the perps in the time we'll gain from them leaving the area."

Benoit received a hand slap from Rosie as Sammy Blackmon wrote down the roadblocks that were effected. Finally he looked up with a smile on his face. "All roadblocks are now taken down and they've take about two dozen investigators with them north. Looks like Memphis is going to be gridlock for a while."

Benoit grinned broadly as the impact of his trick sunk in. "We have a lot of work to do. Rosie, get over to that bar again and see if the owner is any more cooperative this time."

He turned to Sammy. "I want you to continue to monitor the channels. You might be the only one who will know when they call off the search up there. I would say we've bought maybe three or four days. Not more."

He looked around the room, then made another decision. "Russell, you take Ben and hightail it over to Pensacola. You need to check out some of those the Feds were interviewing. We need to know everything they told our law enforcement brethren."

Ben raised the question on everyone's mind. "And what are you going to do, Boss?"

Benoit rubbed his head for a moment. "I think I shall go over to the Sheriff's office and offer my services. Might be able to shake something out."

14 SNEAKING IN THE BACK WAY

Clint Black came back into the dilapidated house and picked up his saddlebags. Dust sifted through sunbeams back onto the floor. Melinda and Desmond both looked up – then grabbed their stuff and followed him out the door. It didn't shut behind them. They got into the muscle car that Clint had hot-wired and left the music city scene behind them.

"Five hours and we'll be back where we belong," Clint remarked as they pulled onto Interstate 55 South. "I trust our good friends at the FBI will have a great time looking for us. Think we left enough clues?"

Desmond sneered as he looked at Southaven disappearing behind them. "They couldn't find their asses if you gave them a hundred clues. Talk about amateurs at the game. They should have picked up on Melinda's face at least and made the connection to the beach party. Maybe the right guy didn't come north."

Talk was suspended for most of the trip. Finally they pulled onto Interstate 10 East and Melinda asked something that was on all their minds. "The Boss hasn't called us in two days. Wonder if he found something?"

Desmond squeezed her close to him and repositioned his body against the small seat in the back of the car. He and his wife had crawled in there earlier to get some sleep while Clint drove. "He wouldn't necessarily try to communicate with us under normal terms. The Feds do have ways of tracking."

Everyone was silent as that thought went through their minds. It was true that once the FBI turned their full resources onto a subject – they usually produced concrete results. Not for the first time all of them were thinking the same thing – why hadn't the Bureau gotten closer to them than they had?

Gulfport soon appeared and disappeared as they drove into Biloxi. No road blocks and when they called into headquarters to check in they found that everything in the area had become quiet. As if everyone were waiting for the Bureau to arrive once more to take up the now cold leads of the case.

Rosie filled them in on the particulars. "The Boss is out at one of the golf courses following up on a lead. He thinks it might be hot, so we're standing by waiting on his report. Ben and Russell and Sammy have just returned from tearing Pensacola apart and are sleeping. Got a wakeup call in for six this evening. What did you guys discover in Memphis?"

"Not much," Desmond admitted as he set his pack down behind the door. "We think the FBI might have bit on our feint a little too hard. Seems they went overboard on taking the bait. Has Benoit said anything about that?"

Rosie sat back on her stool and frowned. "As a matter of fact that was the discussion around here last night. The Boss thinks that maybe they bit a little too hard himself. Said it wasn't a mistake that he would have made. That's why he has approached this intelligence gathering with extra caution and advised me to instruct you three to lay low and get some rest. We might be looking at a double feint. Not likely but also not to be on the old discounted list."

Desmond and Melinda went to their room and Clint crashed on the couch. The house fell silent again except for the comms station – which monitored both the Sheriff's office and the Feds. There was nothing newsworthy coming across it and Rosie kind of dozed a couple times as the afternoon waned.

In the meantime, Ronald Benoit was beating the bushes around the A.J. Holloway Sports Complex. He had discovered that one of the groundskeepers for the city golf course was on the FBI's most wanted list.

Earl Benson had been placed on the list because he failed to produce sufficient documentation when they stopped him at one of the routine stops. His whereabouts became unknown right after the traffic stop. Benoit found his address during a foray into the offices of the golf course the night before.

He was standing inside the man's trailer – letting his eyes adjust to the dimness inside the trailer. No evidence of breathing or movement – so no one was home. He took out his flashlight and began a systematic rummage through the trailer. Finally he left the Cedar Ridge Mobile Home facility behind him and drove back to the safe house.

The briefing went smoothly that evening as the entire crew got up to speed on the circumstances as they now stood. Benoit filled them in on what he had found at the trailer. "The man is a certain pedophile. Those are the shots that I took of various objects in his trailer. I think he is one of our perps but he is still flying under the radar. We have to find him. Then he will turn over the others. I'm sure of it."

The entire team was silent for a long time as they considered the intel they had just received. The fate of those who had already been murdered and the fate of those who could still be in danger was on the minds of each of them.

"We begin tomorrow to draw in the noose around these guys. I want everyone rested so we can concentrate fully on the mission and what we have to do to complete it. Any qualms regarding our instructions?"

No response. Everyone was on board with their mission and no one had any second thoughts about it. Benoit went to his cot and fell into a deep sleep. Everyone else followed suit. Tomorrow was going to be a fun day of following leads.

15 CASE #605 – RANDI SOMERS

Randi Somers flipped her blonde hair back over her shoulder and strutted into Starbucks as a guy held the door for her. She knew people were looking at the way she had been painted into her skinny jeans. Her size 36 bra poked through the sheer fabric of her white blouse – enhancing the mood she had walked in with. She was the center of attention.

She smiled sweetly at the guy behind the counter and Jason almost melted from her attention. Randi certainly realized what happened to most guys when she turned her baby blues in their direction. Jason Grishom was no exception. His palms began to sweat as he tried to concentrate on what she was saying.

"I want a skinny, non-fat latte. Hold the foam and make it sweet. And a date to the Fall Dance in two weeks. Can you arrange that?" She smacked her lips, tasting the pink icing lip gloss she had applied in the car – expecting him to say yes right away.

He didn't and she began to feel her blood boil. Jason shook his head. "I don't date high school girls."

"And I don't date morons! I am twenty years old. High school my ass! You better be glad I asked you out anyway. Cancel the latte and the rest of your miserable life."

She turned around and stomped out of the coffee shop. She didn't see the two guys who had been in line behind her as they rushed to their car and followed her out of the parking area.

She turned left on Highway 49 and headed down to 13th Street where she worked at the Half Shell – serving up oysters on the half shell to businessmen who had blown into town for the weekend. She surveyed the crowd as she tied on her apron. It had already become busy and it was just past 11:00 am. She sighed and tried to put the fiasco at the coffee shop far from her mind.

Earl and Rico came in a few minutes later and stayed a while – not eating much but trying to start up a conversation with her. She eventually went into the back to avoid them and they were gone when she returned to the floor.

Something about those two gave her the creeps. One of them had the look of a predator in his eyes and she certainly didn't want to meet the swarthy one in a dark alley. He just had hard core criminal written all over him. Randi shuddered as she remembered their eyes following her across the restaurant floor. She couldn't help it.

She forgot about them by 7:00 pm as her shift came to an end. She was now looking forward to hooking up with her friends, Britney and Chloe. They would rock someone's world until the wee hours of the morning and then crash on someone's couch or bed until it was time to get up and do it again. She was glad that she thought ahead and had extra clothes in the car.

She did not pick up on the fact that an old beat up van was following close behind her as she headed for her house to freshen up before joining her friends. It drove on past as she parked on the street. Randi paid it no mind and didn't notice that it parked down the street. She rushed up to her door and turned the key to let herself inside.

Disaster struck. Rico slammed her up against the door and forced it open. Randi stumbled as he pushed her inside and would have fallen if he hadn't grabbed her around the waist. He pulled her hard back into him and she smelled the same stale cigar scent she had noticed at the restaurant. Her blood froze as she realized who was holding onto her.

She shrieked but it did nothing except get her backhanded on the back of her head. Her brains seemed to jiggle and sharp pain went through her neck as he tightened his grip on her.

Randi was having a hard time breathing. Rico pushed her up against the wall and wasted no time telling her what he wanted. Ice was forming in her veins as she listened to him.

"You can't be serious," she stammered as he slammed her back into the wall. "I will never do that for you and you can't make me." She tried to kick him but he backhanded her. This time she blacked out for a moment and woke up on the floor.

She raised herself up on her forearms and tried to shake her head to clear the cobwebs. Rico took that moment to thrust her onto her back and sit on her. The breath was knocked out of her lungs again and she gasped with pain as his knees dug into her sides.

Rico pulled his switchblade from his hip pocket and pointed it at her throat. "Scream again and I'll do you from here to here." He pointed the knife at each side of her pretty throat and gloated when the fear really set into her eyes.

"You see? You can make a good decision when you have to. Earl there knows I like a little fight in my women, but let's be reasonable. There is a limit to the noise I can take."

He stood up and pointed the knife at her jeans. "Get them off before I decide to cut you out of them. This trusty old knife might slip in the process and score some cuts along your torso. Wouldn't want that, now would we?"

Randi hurried to do what he wanted and lay there in her black and white panty – trying to cover up as best she could. But he left her no choice as he spread her legs wide and knelt between them. She closed her eyes and tried to ignore the fact that he was having his way with her body.

A big man came in as Rico was finishing up and took his place. Randi felt as if they had thrust a two by four inside her. The man was big and rough. She had never felt so used in all her life. He eventually finished and the man called Earl took his place and she was well and truly raped by the time he was finished.

Then Rico was back. It was like he hadn't finished earlier and he built up a full head of steam. "Why aren't you enjoying this?" he inquired.

She spat. "You might possess my body but you can't have my soul, you pig! I will never enjoy this for you. You've wasted your time. I'll never be yours!"

Rico thrust the knife under her chin – up into her brain case as he finished his business. Then he wiped off the knife on her silk blouse and pulled up his trousers.

"Get everything together and let's get out of here. Take everything that ain't locked down. Old Volgamore likes our business and we aim to please."

They left Randi laying in the middle of the floor and made off with her booty. Things had come together well for the team.

16 TAUNTING AUTHORITIES

Rico turned over on the couch where he had been trying to sleep for the past couple hours. Sleep wouldn't come and he finally admitted something was wrong and sat up. He scratched the stubble on his chin as the first smoke of the day filtered through the air of the darkened living room.

He could hear snoring coming from the bedroom and knew his companions were logged out of life for a while. Both had complained of how tired they were. Rico guessed that good fucking probably took it out of you. He wouldn't know – his pleasure wasn't in the carnality of the moment – just the infliction of pain and suffering.

His mother's shrink had said that Rico was a 'walking time bomb who would end up hurting a lot of people.' He had proved the old man correct. Dr. Snyder had said he was a sociopath – that he was. He had used other big words that described all of the worst qualities of Rico's life and at the young age of fourteen Rico had begun living up to those qualities.

His mother had died horribly – along with Dr. Snyder. Rico had positioned their bodies so the police thought they were illicit lovers. He still chuckled from the way they had looked as he left out the back door and never returned. But he did follow the investigation until the police dropped the case into the Cold Case box and forgot about it. Rico never forgot about it – in fact, that cold case drove his every waking moment. He couldn't cause enough pain to get past it.

Nor could he gain enough notoriety to suit him. Earl said they didn't need to rub the nose of the police in their ineptitude but he was wrong.

Rico stiffened as the thoughts finally struck home. That was exactly what they needed to do. Make the police feel stupid for not having caught up with them. By now they should have. Rico was conscious that they had the manpower to do it. And he was aware of the FBI and their wanderings throughout the southern landscape. By now they should have gained some real insight into the case and be hot on their trail. That didn't appear to be the case.

"Well, we are gonna have to change that," he said with a finality that boded ill for the other members of his team. He took out the cell phone he had kept from one of the crime scenes and dialed the number for the local Sheriff.

"Hello, you don't know me." He paused. "I have some information on the guys who are raping all those girls."

"Hold on sir while I get my manager on the phone."

A moment later Deputy Morgan Smith picked up the line. "Who did you say you are?"

"Never mind that. I am your worst nightmare and I'm not going away. More of your darling daughters and mothers are going to suffer and die at the hands of my men. We are taking our revenge on the lusting whores of your fair city. Nothing personal. We just wanted to tell you how foolish you look with all your running around and chasing your tails."

Deputy Morgan snapped his fingers to get the attention of the others in the room. One of them sprang to the tracing station and punched in the number he wrote down. They began the trace that might give them the first break they had had in the case.

"Why are you doing this?"

"Oh, you mean calling you? Or the rape and murder?"

"Why are you doing both? And what do you want from the Sheriff?"

"Oh," again Rico paused. "I want to turn myself and my partners in. But not to you guys. I want the director of the FBI himself to come down here and take me in. No one else – you hear? Just the director. Otherwise we will walk out of here and be long gone. Personally, I can take up my profession anywhere. Good luck finding me."

"Wait, how do I know you are the one involved in the murders?"

"You no doubt are aware that none of the girls had their panties removed."

"Yes, and we're also aware that there were at least three sets of DNA at each crime scene. What does that prove?"

"The last girl had a sharp object driven up into her brain."

Deputy Morgan felt ice crystal beginning to form in his gut. The police had not released that information to the public. He knew he was talking to the perpetrator. "Please stay on the line and I will get the Sheriff to speak with you."

"And allow you to triangulate my location? I don't think so. Just call this number back when the director is ready."

Rico hung up and left the deputy stammering. He then ran into the bedroom and switched on the light. "Get up you two buffoons!" he shouted. "The police are on their way here even as you snooze your lives away! Get dressed and let's split."

Both guys were in a turmoil that only settled down as they piled into the car and made their escape.

17 RUNNING FROM THE LAW

Sheriff Jerome Tackett ducked under the yellow tape and stepped into the abandoned apartment. His spider sense was all a tingling as he surveyed the scene. Someone had departed in a very big hurry from the looks of it. Clothes and toiletries were left behind in their panic to vacate the premises before the police arrived.

"This place doesn't play well with the tip we got, does it Sir?"

Tackett looked sideways at his deputy while his eyes still swept across the bedroom. His quarry had obviously been in a hurry to leave. His deputy was correct in his assumption. Something just didn't ring true about the phone call or the premises. Tackett had the feeling that he was being played.

"At least one of them wanted us to pick up their trail," he stated as he walked into the kitchen. A large bin was full of pizza delivery box and there was debris of previous meals all over the untidy counters.

"Get someone in here to bag and tag this mess. And Morgan?"

"Yes sir."

"Don't discuss this place with anyone. We don't want the Feds to get wind that we are on the trail of our murder suspects. You got that?"

"Yes, sir. How do you want me to call it in?"

"Tell them Little Red Riding Hood has been found." Tackett threw his hands up in exasperation. Sometimes his deputy couldn't think for himself or get on the same page. "Think of something, damn it! Just get this place taken care of. I've got to get on their trail before it goes cold."

The Sheriff walked back out to his car and sat for a couple minutes considering his next steps in the pursuit. It was obvious to him that someone wanted somebody caught. He didn't quite know how to go about the catching while at the same time keeping his law enforcement brethren in the dark. Really no sense in allowing them to take all the glory.

His thoughts centered on how to instruct his staff without giving anything away. He was certain that by now the FBI had listening devices all over his precinct. He took his cell phone from his breast pocket and dialed a number.

Maggie Barnard answered after a couple rings. "Don't say a word, just listen. Margaret Ann, you need pancakes and coffee." He hung up and started his engine.

Halfway across town Desmond spoke into his headset. "Boss, the Sheriff just sent their dispatcher out for food. Something about pancakes and coffee."

Benoit keyed his mike – responding without a word. He put his bike into gear and followed the Sheriff at a safe distance. The location turned out to be a Denny's on Route 49 – along the beach. Benoit parked in the lot and activated the transmitter in the Sheriff's phone.

"What's this all about?" Maggie asked as they sat down. She had never seen the Sheriff in such a state of nerves.

"Remember that phone call we got this morning?"

She nodded. "You mean the one with the creepy voice?"

"Yeah. That's the one. We followed up and something is weird."

"In what way weird?" Maggie was definitely puzzled.

"The person who called wants us to follow them. They left in a hurry out of the place we raided and left everything behind. Not likely if they weren't in a god-awful hurry. Sounds to me like we need to set up unofficial roadblocks and see if we can't drag them in. I want you to bring in everyone who isn't on duty and have them looking for an old beat-up pickup. License plate is Florida BNC154Y. Tell them to call it in as a routine traffic stop if they do encounter and then pass it directly to me."

Maggie sat back and smiled. "You aren't keying the Feds into this one – are you, sir?"

"No, Maggie. I'm not. They can arrive from their trip up north to find we already have the perps in custody. But we don't want anyone tipping them off before we land them in the net. Your job will be secured for quite a few years from the funds we can net from this one arrest. Is that good enough reason for playing coy?"

Maggie set her coffee cup back down and looked the Sheriff in the eye. "We have the manpower to do this. I'll brief them all before they hit the road. How far away do you think they are?"

"If I'm right – they didn't leave the area. I'd say they are trying to hide in plain sight. So be aware of any calls that come in. We don't want to miss anything."

"Okay, Sheriff. Where are you going to be?"

"Only a phone call away, Maggie." He patted his cell phone, dropped a ten dollar bill on the table and left. Maggie finished her coffee and split. Things were in the works and she had a lot of work to do to make the Sheriff's plan happen.

18 CASE FILE #712

At the young age of 15, Jeanie Sherman was too grown up for her age. She had worn makeup since the fifth grade and had been making out with boys since she was ten. Her mother didn't seem to mind that she attracted the wrong sort of male friends. In fact, her mother didn't mind about a lot of things since Jeanie had thought to introduce her to some of her younger home-boys.

Misha Sherman had split from Jeanie's father when Jeanie was three years old. She had sworn off men because of their tendency to cheat. She thought all men were dogs. All men were going to cheat on her and she was determined not to get involved with any of them.

That vow was kept religiously for a number of years – until her daughter was thirteen. On a sultry day in September of that year she almost walked in to discover her daughter involved not with one guy but two. Misha stepped back out of the room and no one noticed she was there.

Jeanie was taking one man doggie style and giving head to the other man. Something in Mom snapped as she watched and listened to her own daughter having sex with two men. She felt a tingling inside her lower belly that she hadn't noticed in years. A timid hand explored inside her short skirt and she found that she was ready to ride the dragon.

That had been weeks in the past. She had made a point of asking Jeanie about her friends and her daughter finally gave in and introduced her to several of them. After that mother and daughter double-teamed a selected cadre of Jeanie's friends and Misha fell further and further into a sex induced stupor.

Jeanie pulled her mother's red Miata into a filling station along the beach between Biloxi and D'lberville. When she stepped out her long legs preceded her and her loose, flared skirt blew with the breeze coming off the ocean. The afternoon was progressing and a glare from the sun blocked her view as she looked back up the coast towards downtown Biloxi.

The main thing she didn't see was the three men who were standing over by an old beat up pickup truck that looked as if it had received its last rites. Rico tapped the big guy on the back and indicated he was to dump the truck on a back street and then join them at their newest hideout.

Then he moved out to the island where Jeanie was parked and tried to start up a conversation.

"You know Kenny G?"

"Who?" She looked at him over the rims of her sun glasses and didn't recognize his face. She tried to blow him off but he persisted nonetheless.

"You know. Kenny G – the DJ over at Roc. I think I've seen you in there dancing a time or two, haven't I?"

Jeanie nodded slightly. Although she had snuck in there with a fake id, she didn't want the whole world to know about it. "Maybe once or twice – as someone's date."

Rico leaned on the pump and watched her intently. "Did he know how old you are?"

"No. And I don't think that is any of your business either. So push off before I call the cops." She placed the nozzle back on the pump and started to tighten her gas cap. She wasn't ready for his hand to cover hers – or his other hand to surround her neck.

She looked fearfully into his eyes and knew the truth that was staring her in the face. She would be lucky to survive the night. She saw rage and ferocity in his eyes and knew she was in trouble. That was really slammed home when her engine started and someone yelled for her assailant to get in the car.

Rico opened the passenger door and forced Jeanie into the back seat and then sat beside her. Earl had to reach across the small car to shut the door. Jeanie found herself on the pointed end of a switchblade.

"Now, you just sit quietly and make no fuss and you might just get through this evening and rejoin your slut of a mother."

In spite of her fear, Jeanie had to ask how he knew her mother. Rico sniggered. "Everyone in these parts has heard how she has taken to entertaining as many as three and four at a time. We've been looking for her. But now we know that you are fresher."

He teased her about her mother all the way back to the latest flop house the gang was using. Then he made her get out at knife point and undress for him as they entered the apartment.

"Come on girl. Do it slowly like you're wanting us to enjoy it."

The next morning Misha Sherman reported that her daughter had not come home and reported her car as stolen. Sheriff Tackett was alerted immediately and the knot in his stomach became a full scale maelstrom. He alerted all the authorities at that point and began working on an amber alert since the missing girl was only fifteen.

He hoped they wouldn't have to place her face on a milk carton for someone to identify. It was going to be a long night and he knew without a doubt that his quarry had not left the area.

19 CASE FILE #713

Barbie Simmons flipped her ponytail and screeched to the top of her lungs as she watched her current boyfriend dunk a basket during their school's rival game with the Gulfport Pirates. That she knew almost nothing about the game meant nothing. She really liked the way Tommy looked in his uniform and she liked fitting in with the older girls who populated the stands.

Barbie would not be a real teenager until next year – a fact which frustrated the hell out of her. But her father kept telling her that she had filled out great for her age. And her mother went out of her way to encourage her daughter to use the right shades on her lips and eyes. Said she could add a couple years with the expert management of her face. Mom had always been great.

Barbie remembered back to the third grade when Mom had made her up one morning before school. The other girls had been so envious that the tradition stuck – in spite of male teachers who said she was a tart and a tease. She had become the one encouraging other girls in their own self illuminations.

Ginny Brooks leaned forward and tapped Barbie on the shoulder. "Your boyfriend is going to want a real woman soon and I know a little secret."

Fear flowed chill through her bones but Barbie tried to make light of Ginny's scathing remarks.

"You don't know anything or you would already have told him." She turned and looked steadily into Ginny's eyes. "Besides, he's going to be getting some of this tonight. Eat your heart out bitch and leave me alone."

Ginny poked one of her friends in the side to get her attention. "Listen to this little mama, will you? She swears she ain't gonna be no virgin by the morning. Want to take bets on where her Tommy puts his meat tonight?"

Half dozen voices blended over the general noise and Tommy looked up from his seat on the bench where he was taking a breather. Barbie looked like she was being besieged by a whole coven of crows. Her face was set and furious. He wondered what was being said but didn't have time to try to find out as the coach called him to get back in the game.

Barbie moved away from the older girls and checked out the concession stand area. She hadn't been there for more than a couple minutes when she was approached by a man who was related to one of the girls who had been picking on her.

Tommy looked for her after the game and ended up getting in over his head with some of the girls who wanted to party. It wasn't until the next morning when he looked around in Algebra and saw that her seat was empty. His blonde girlfriend wasn't there – nor did she answer his calls or text. That was strange.

Around dismissal an assistant principal announced over the intercom that there was an Amber Alert that had been issued but Tommy wasn't really listening and it was a real shock when a patrol car pulled up in his driveway while he was walking home.

"Are you Tommy Beach?" a uniformed patrolwoman asked him as he turned up his drive. He nodded and tried to move past her partner – a big hulk of a character who sported a scar down his right cheek that slightly pulled his mouth out of kilter.

"Answer the officer," he growled as he stepped further into Tommy's lane in such a way that Tommy would be forced to step in his mother's flower bed to avoid him. He wasn't going to do that so he stopped.

"Are you going to allow me to pass?" he inquired softly.

"As soon as you answer the lady. Are you Tommy Beach?"

"Yes, officer. I am and I'm certain my mother would like to know why you're trying to question me without her knowledge."

He stared into the patrolman's eyes for a couple moments and then decided not to continue to challenge the man. The hulk's partner moved them past the awkward moments and suggested they go into the house to continue their conversation.

Tommy went into the back of the house to get his mother and they both listened carefully to the policewoman.

"Your son went to a basketball game last night with a young girl who goes to his school. Did you know that, Ma'am?"

"I knew he had a ball game last night. I wasn't aware he was taking anyone to it. After all, last night was a school night."

"What time did he get home from the game?"

"I had to get up early this morning so I went to sleep around nine o'clock. He usually gets a shower there and gets home before ten. That's an arrangement we have. He doesn't abuse the privilege of playing on a school night by getting in at a decent hour."

"Did you know he was out with a minor last night?"

Tommy's eyes went wide as he met his mother's. She blinked and looked back at the policewoman.

"What are you saying? That my son had something to do with that Amber Alert they've been announcing on the TV? You didn't, did you?" She turned toward Tommy.

He stammered and tried to catch his breath. "I don't know what they're talking about," he protested.

The big patrolman took out his notebook and checked it, then remarked, "I guess she didn't tell you how old she was, huh?"

"No, she didn't. We've only been seeing each other at school for a couple weeks. Last night was the first real date we been on and she left before the game was over."

"You didn't wonder why?"

"Yes. Of course I wondered and I looked all over the place for her. I did. I swear to you Mom I looked for her."

"Then what?"

"I decided she must have gotten a ride home and I came on home myself."

"Did you walk with anyone?"

"No. I was alone."

The big guy took over. "Well, whereas you arrived home, a twelve year old girl did not. She was with you and then she wasn't. We need to account for your whereabouts."

Tommy glanced over again at his mother. He was stunned and she could tell he hadn't known the girl was twelve. "I swear I didn't know she was that age. I would never have even talked with her if I'd known. She looks much older."

"We're going to need you to come down to the station to assist us with finding her, if you don't mind."

Mrs. Beach grabbed her jacket and keys. "I'm coming with you."

20 AMBER ALERT ISSUED

Desmond took his headphones off and looked across the room where his wife had just set down a basket of laundry that she had retrieved from the laundromat across the street. "Minda, we have to get in touch with the Boss fast!"

Melinda Howard's eyes narrowed. She knew that tone and also recognized the tense look on his features. Their twelve years of marriage gave insight into her husband. She reached for her cell phone and immediately dialed Ronald Benoit's number – while her husband returned his head phones to his ears as he hurriedly scribbled some notes on one of the pads at their listening station.

"Tell him the local cops have just put out an Amber Alert that he was looking for. On a twelve year old female named Barbie Simmons. Local Leo's talked with her mother this morning and they have put out the alert without calling in the Feds. Tell Ronald there is a boy involved that he police have already interviewed once. He kind of took her to a basketball game Tuesday night and didn't go home with her."

He paused as Melinda filled in the blanks for Benoit – who was with Clint out on the other side of the Air Force base – going through some of the things they had been able to remove from a previous crime scene.

"The him the boy's name is Tommy Beach. He lives at 1689 Sandford Place. That's about 10 miles from his present location. He and Clint can be there inside five minutes."

Benoit listened carefully and then gave orders for Sammy and Rose to join Clint. He was dispatching the three of them in hopes of being able to pick up a trail of some sort leading from the boy to the Simmons girl. They probably didn't have more than six hours left to find the girl. Maybe not even that – if the current profile was still a workable one.

Somehow he had the feeling that things had changed. At first the perps had been intent on raping, killing and stealing. Now it seemed they wanted to keep the victim alive until they no longer needed them or as insurance against being cornered by the cops. Benoit scratched his head as he continued looking through the items they had removed from the crime scene of Jeanie Sherman.

He was still puzzled when Clint called to report that the local cops had the boy's house staked out. "We can't even get into the house from the rear garden. They have someone inside in the kitchen and the boy and his mother are being held under what amounts to house arrest until the Sheriff shows up. We were able to listen in on their conversation."

"Well done. Desmond was telling me the locals have shut up when it comes to the radio. Maybe they found one of our bugs and think the Feds have them under surveillance. That would probably spook anyone. I've sent Des and Melinda to the girl's house to see if there is anything happening there. Should know something shortly. Are you in a place where you can maintain your cover?"

"We are. You want us to stay here a while, I take it."

"Yes, we need to find out how much the boy actually knows and what he has told Tackett's deputies. I'm certain he probably knows more than he told them. Hang tight until I call back."

Clint pulled his hoodie down over his forehead and informed his team of Benoit's decision. "Let's hope something breaks soon."

Benoit and the Howards were thinking exactly the same thing. If they couldn't catch a break in the case soon – they all feared the girl would be found dead. It wasn't like the perps to be patient, but it was like they enjoyed messing with the lawman's head.

Sheriff Tackett showed up right after Melinda had reported that there also was a police presence at the girl's house. Front and back were covered and very little could be heard inside the house – though Desmond had tried.

Clint listened in on Tackett as he grilled the young man again and spelled out in no uncertain terms what would happen to him if he was found to be withholding evidence. The boy cracked and Clint sighed with relief. They might have just gotten their first real tangible break in the case.

"Boss, the boy just admitted he spent the night over at some girl's house on Lockhart Avenue. 1456 Lockhart. That should be about three miles from where you're at. Tackett hasn't called anyone yet so it looks like he plans to take care of it himself. I think you probably have time to beat him to the punch."

"Roger that. I'm on my way. You continue listening in and keep me apprised of when he leaves."

Ginny Brooks was getting ready to go out clubbing when Benoit knocked on the door. Her mother answered the door and stood in shock once he had explained why he wanted to talk with her daughter. Ginny's outfit made her mother blush when she bounced down the stairs."

"Momma, I'm going over to Charlotte's for a study group," she said as she turned to the full length mirror in the hall and pranced down off the bottom step. She stopped sudden as she recognized there was someone else in the room.

"What's going on?" she demanded as she slipped her London Fog over her shoulders. She looked at the man talking with her mother and decided she couldn't judge whether he was from the school or the cops. The cops had been up and down their street asking if anyone had seen that foolish little girl. Maybe that's what it was about.

Her mother made the introduction. "Honey, this is Mr. Monk. He is with the Child Alert task force and is asking questions about that little girl who was kidnapped earlier. You know, the one on the news who you said you went to school with. That one. He wants to ask you some questions about her and I said he could."

Ginny shrugged. "I barely know who you're talking about. I don't have any classes with her so she doesn't move in the same circles as the upper class at the school."

Benoit got right to the point. "But you were seen talking to her the other night at a basketball game. Tommy Beach also said that he saw you talking to her. Then he later spent the night with you instead of taking her home."

Ginny's face flushed. "Well, he's a liar! I didn't see her at the game because I was over at my friend's house studying for a big test. And I certainly didn't spend any time with that loser! He is trying to get out of taking her home by blaming me. It's a lie!"

Benoit wasn't going to let a few croc tears daunt his investigation. "No, I think he is telling the truth finally. Sheriff Tackett will be over here shortly to take you downtown to answer some questions. He is really interested in finding Barbie Simmons and they know you had something to do with her disappearance."

He turned toward her mother. "Mrs. Brooks, please. Tackett seems to think that your daughter had something to do with the girl's disappearance and he isn't going to come in here with kid's gloves on, if you know what I mean. My agency can protect her, if you'll allow us and keep Tackett off your back. But both of you will have to be put under Federal custody as soon as possible."

She made up her mind real quick. "Let me get my coat and keys, Mr. Monk."

Benoit led them out to his car and they drove away moments before Tackett's men showed up to block off the street. The Sheriff showed up about fifteen minutes later to find out his prize witness had disappeared. His signature hat was stomped into the late Autumn mud and his bluest language filled the air.

21 BIKER GANG ROUNDUPS

Ronald Benoit was trying to rest his eyes after being out in the bright sunshine along the beach. He had returned to the scene of the first murder to see if there might have been something that had been overlooked during the initial investigation. There wasn't. Now he was sitting on a wooden bench in one of the gazeboes that lined the beach – listening with his eyes closed as the tide came sneaking back in.

His phone buzzed and disturbed his reverie. 'This better be something good,' he thought as he dug it out of his pocket. Desmond Howard's voice brought him to full awareness.

"Mildred, I've been picked up and charged. Melinda and Clint are with me and this is my one phone call."

Benoit's eyes narrowed. The code word Mildred sparked his mind into high gear. It meant the local police had picked them up and that they were being held for interrogation. The reference to the one phone call meant they hadn't been taken to the interview room yet. Maybe he still had time.

Benoit looked at his watch and nodded. It was after five o'clock – normally shift change for the local Leo's. He could get into the station during their most lax time and possibly get them released into federal custody.

Picking a federal badge from his stash, he hurried out to the official, black SUV they had kept just for the occasion.

Ten minutes later he walked into the local precinct and showed his badge to the policewoman on duty at the desk. She barely looked up and seemed to be paying more attention to the logging in of about a dozen bikers who had just been brought into the station.

"Uh, you'll have to talk to Sheriff Tackett before you can see any of the prisoners. He's in the second office down the hall. But he's getting ready to do some interviews so you might have to wait."

Benoit acknowledged and slid down the left hand hallway. He saw Tackett come out of his office and hurry in the direction of the interrogation rooms. He had a bunch of manila folders in his hand and looked like his hair was on fire.

Ronald followed him to the door of the nearest room and the Sheriff turned around to look at him. "Who are you?" he demanded impatiently.

"I'm Chief Inspector Morse, FBI."

The Sheriff looked him over – trying to assess whether he was being had on or what. "I'm about to begin a very important interview and don't really have time to answer any questions you might have. Come by my office in the morning."

"I'm afraid that won't do, Sheriff. The people you are about to interview are my people and I'm afraid I can't allow you to conduct this interview."

Sheriff Tackett felt his blood pressure rise and his neck and face began to show the splotches of frustration he was already beginning to feel.

"Where the hell do you get off coming into my station and telling me I can't interview suspects?"

"Because they aren't suspects, Sheriff. They are undercover agents who have been looking for the people who have been doing the murders and kidnappings you are investigating. Now you need to release them."

"I will do no such thing!" The Sheriff pumped up another inch and tried to intimidate Benoit. It didn't work and he finally broke off the staring contest and asked to see Benoit's badge again. Ronald also produced a memorandum that laid out his instructions as an FBI investigator.

The Sheriff glanced into the room and gestured to one of his interrogators. "Release them. They're free to go."

Benoit stood aside as his people exited the room to recover their property.

"You will keep me apprised of anything you find while you're in my jurisdiction, won't you?"

"Of course, Sheriff. We are working the same side of crime here. I'll keep you informed. Just tell your men not to harass my people during the investigation. And I will take you up on the invitation to visit your office in the morning. Thanks"

Benoit walked out and followed his men. Sheriff Tackett was left scratching his head but quickly got into the swing of things as more bikers were brought into the interview rooms.

22 INTERROGATION

Earl Benson had been drinking quietly in the Forbidden Lizard Lounge when the police broke in and conducted a raid. He had never been locked up before so he didn't have any idea of what to expect. His turn came to walk into the Interrogation Room and his vital signs spiked through the roof.

"For the record, say your name and give us your address and date of birth." The lady detective on the other side of the desk was a looker, but Earl didn't really have time to appreciate her.

"Uh, Earl Benson. 12/02/1979. I currently live with my mother on Elm Street."

"What is the address, sir?"

"Oh, 5637 Elm."

"What were you doing in the Forbidden Lizard, Mr. Benson?"

"I was drinking. Is that a crime?"

"Don't be sarcastic, Mr. Benson. We are trying to interview people who could have seen a serial killer and the Lizard is one place we know that they have been seen. Why were you there last night?"

"Because I wanted a drink and it is around the corner from my mother's house. That's why."

"Do you often go in there alone?"

"As a matter of fact, I do. I like the ambiance. And the quiet way they go about doing business in there. Is that a crime now?"

"Only if you frequently associate with certain know criminal elements while you're in there. Mr. Benson, we have it on good report that you were seen drinking with two other men in there at least twice in the last two weeks. Who were they?"

"I don't know," Earl shrugged his shoulders. "They came in one evening and we played some pool. Never saw them before that night and neither one gave his name."

"So what did the three of you do? Remember, Mr. Benson that you are under oath and can be bound over to the Grand Jury if we believe you are lying or withholding evidence during our inquiry. You do understand that?"

Earl ducked his head. "Yes, ma'am. I understand. But I didn't catch any names?"

"Is that because they didn't need to introduce themselves to you? Isn't it true that you already knew them?"

"No! That is not true. I hadn't seen them before that night and have only played pool with them one time since. They just come in, drink and play. Then they leave. I don't know anything more than that. They are a real mystery to me."

His interrogator looked at her notes and scribbled a couple of her own, then looked his straight in the eyes. "Mr. Benson. Did they say anything about what they do, where they work or where they live?"

Earl shook his head, laid his palms flat on the table and tried desperately to calm his breathing. "They only said they worked with tires. I think at least the big guy works at a garage somewhere out toward Pensacola. But that's all I know."

"You haven't really been all that helpful, Mr. Benson. We picked you up in a bar where these two criminals have been seen and you want us to believe you don't know either of them?"

Earl shrugged again. "I can only tell you what I know. You act like you want me to make something up. I'm the innocent one here and you're just fishing for something to nail me with. I want a lawyer."

"And one will be provided for you. Mr. Benson, you do know that you can be charged with kidnapping and murder charges. Does that help you remember anything?"

Shaking his head, Earl again requested his lawyer. The interview session ended and he was taken back to a holding cell. The policewoman rubbed her temple vigorously and admitted she didn't have a clue about the man. "Maybe he is just an innocent who was in the wrong place at the right time. I don't know. We probably will have to let him go and put a tail on him."

23 OUT ON BAIL

Earl walked out of the police station. A free man. Some bail bondsman had showed up and Earl was walking free. He flipped his keys in the air as his bike was brought out of the impound yard. Another flick and he was on his way down 18th Street – getting ready to turn onto Highway 49 heading east.

The sun was just starting to peek above the horizon when he turned onto Interstate 10 and headed for Pensacola. He cranked the bike to 95 and cruised. The bailiff had told him not to leave Biloxi but he didn't care. The gang needed to know what was in store for them if and when they got picked up.

Earl didn't bother to look behind him. A black Harley was creeping closer with every mile and a nondescript police cruiser was in front of it. Desmond and Melinda Howard pretended to be taking in the sights as they cruised. The trio in the cruiser didn't pay them any mind and the group steadily headed eastward.

Pensacola came into view and Earl turned onto one of the back streets off one of the main boulevards. Desmond slowed down but didn't make the turn. Melinda kept the bike in sight and punched him in the side when it turned into a driveway about half way down the street. Desmond gunned the bike and noted the cruiser was turning in behind them. He had guessed correctly way back down the road. They were the tail

The cruiser drove down the lane and then parked on the opposite side of the street. That eliminated a couple choices.

Desmond and Melinda conferred and both realized they weren't going to be given the option of driving past the house where Earl had gone to ground. They sat still where they were and waited for Earl to make the next move.

It came about an hour later when a dark green Camero pulled into the drive next door and four people got out and went into the house next door.

"They've obviously got some way set up to go in the back door without anyone knowing," Melinda whispered.

Desmond nodded and suggested they see if there was an alley behind the houses. He turned the bike around and they went to investigate. A couple minutes later they faced a high privacy fence that separated the alley from the back yards.

Melinda dismounted and checked for breaks in the fence. She finally came back over. "There is an opening about four houses down. We can get in there. But there are two dogs between us and the house we need to get into."

"Then I will have to take care of them." He took a pack of hot dogs that he had brought for just that purpose. Two dogs apiece and the guard dogs would be snoozing – not guarding. He set out swiftly to complete his mission and Melinda waited by the opening in the fence. Five minutes passed and Desmond showed up again and gestured for her to follow.

Inside the house in question a low key argument was beginning to heat up. "You've brought at least three cops down on our heads," Rico stated as he looked out an opening in the blinds. "They've parked right over across the street and are just waiting for us to make our next move. You really fucked up this time, old son."

Earl grabbed the tufts of hair behind his ears and tried not to scream. "You weren't there. They grilled me about you and I didn't tell them a thing. They finally let me go back to my cell and then someone showed up and said I was free to go."

"And your good Samaritan was who?"

Earl looked dumbfounded. He hadn't thought about that. "I just thought it was you," he screamed and stomped out of the room.

"I should have strangled him when he came out of his mother! I swear I will take care of him now." Knoff stepped between him and the kitchen but didn't say anything. Rico tried to push past him but there was no budging Knoff when he decided to do something.

Rico finally got the message that he wasn't going to lay hands on Earl and went back to the front window. The street was clear except for the agents he had noticed earlier. No other cars came up or down the street and his blood pressure began to bottom out. He sighed finally and asked Knoff to find Earl.

"You should have been asking who provided the bail money," he said as Earl followed Knoff back into the room. "We are vulnerable when we don't know who all the players are. That's how we've managed to stay one step ahead of the cops all this time. I knew who the players were. Now we don't."

"I'm sorry," Earl replied. "I was so glad to get out of there that I probably wasn't thinking. It won't happen again." He looked around and then took a seat over behind the front door where he could pull the curtain aside to view a good portion of the street. "What do we do now?"

Rico pondered for a while, then answered. "We split them up. That's what we do. Make them chase their tails before any more of them arrive. Earl, you will go to the Naval base and draw them onto the base. You still have that sticker on your car. Should get you through security. Then head back to the bayou and wait for us. We will make sure you aren't being tailed. Now git!"

Earl hurried out the front door and made sure he was being followed as he headed back for the rendezvous point. The Howards' just got back into hiding as Rico and his crew jumped the fence in the back yard and raced through the house to their car as the cops chased after Earl. Desmond sprinted back to his bike and Melinda jumped on. They followed after Rico and Melinda updated the troops on their whereabouts.

24 WITH A TAIL

Rico hadn't been totally honest with Earl about the getaway strategy. Yes, Earl had a car with a Navy sticker on the windshield but the Navy had quit using the stickers and had gone to ID cards for admission onto their bases. Earl didn't have one. The gate guard pulled his weapon and asked Earl to get out of his car. He was had – again.

From Earl's point of view things couldn't have gotten much worse. His perspective wasn't improved much when the lawmen who had followed approached the gate and conferred with the guard. Earl was surprised when the guard came back and ordered him to turn his car around and leave the base.

Earl wasn't surprised when his tail picked up where they had left off. They were forcing him to either approach the rendezvous point or make a break for it and run. He was approaching Interstate 90 when his mind was made up for him. Rico sent a text telling him not to come to the meeting place.

Earl turned west and floored it. To no avail – the police cruiser stayed right on his tail and after he passed into Alabama flipped on their lights and announced for him to pull over. Earl tried to ignore them so they pulled up beside him and steadily moved him over off the road. Earl stopped with a Glock pointed at him head from the rolled down window of the police cruiser. This time he got out of the car and was spread over the hood of his car and handcuffed.

Rico, for his part, had headed straight for the bayou and the gang's hideout. He arrived just before darkness fell across the water and noted the rest of the boys were already there – except Earl, of course. He didn't waste any time thinking about Earl – but might have had he realized that the cops who picked him up were actually Feds instead of local boys. Earl was going to talk.

The Howards snuck into the bayou and rested after seeing Rico go into the ramshackle cabin. There appeared no reason to get any closer and in a conversation with Benoit decided to just remain out of site until the Boss arrived with reinforcements.

Nine o'clock saw them roll into the campground. They set up their tents like any other campers out having a good time and proceeded to observe. D'lberville Bayou Campground had perhaps a dozen areas where bikers could set up sleeping quarters of the transportable type so Benoit had his crew set one up close to the cabin and another down at the exit to the park. Rico wasn't going to get past them in the middle of the night.

Rico was nervous and pacing the floor. Knoff had brought Donny Brooks and Eric Riley – in addition to their latest victim – Barbie Simmons. Rico was furious over that.

"You guys could have dumped her body anywhere." He turned on Knoff. "You idiots didn't have the common sense to dump the bitch?"

Knoff looked like he had been hit. "You didn't tell us to do her, Rico. That is always your responsibility. You know that. I wasn't gonna take it on myself to do that and we knew we couldn't just let her go."

"You're damned right you couldn't!" Rico continued pacing the floor. "We have a problem now. If the police find her with us we face kidnapping charges. That can get you fifteen to life."

Eric spoke for the first time. "Can't we use her as a hostage? You know, to get out of here if they show up?"

Rico's sinister grin split his face in half – the upper part containing a set of steely eyes that cut right through anyone capable of holding eye contact with him.

"All of you are fools!" he spat as he walked over and knelt down beside their captive. "We can't be caught with her. Knoff, you go out and get me that shovel out of the truck and go dig a hole back of the shack. Make it deep enough to cover her. Eric, you go with him and do some of the digging. We need to leave here tonight. So get a move on while I have a little fun."

Clint looked over at Benoit at that point. He removed the headphones and relayed what was happening in the cabin. "He's going to kill her for sure."

Benoit made his decision right away. "Russell, you come with me as soon as the two men go around the side of the house. We go in and get the girl. Knock out Rico and the other man in there with some gas and we get back out of here."

"You don't want to take them out?"

"Not right now. Just put them to sleep and we can pick them up later when we have the van here. Clint, let me know if he hurts the girl."

Clint went back to listening. "He's raping her right now. If it holds as his previous raping he will cut her throat after he ejaculates."

Knoff and Eric went around the building and Benoit indicated they were to move in. Russell dropped the gas into an open window and it puffed. They went inside and found Rico slumped over the girl. Another man was lying beside the door to one of the bedrooms.

Benoit quickly gathered up the girl and slipped out the front door as Russell closed it behind them. They hurried to the tent that had been pitched by the exit and placed her inside. Melinda administered a wakeup drug to her and sat back to make sure she didn't make any noise as she came to.

Benoit went back to the listening post and was informed that Knoff had re-entered the cabin and found Rico knocked out and the girl gone. "Start packing things up and let's get out of here," he instructed as it was obvious things could get nasty if Knoff decided to be a hero.

"We don't want this situation to get out of hand."

25 SHAKING THE FEDS

Rico was groggy when he came to. He was also having vicious thoughts as he glanced across the room and saw the other four men just sitting around. Eric and Knoff were having a soft confab and Donny Brooks looked about as green as Rico felt.

He tried to stand and his stomach revolted until he vomited violently in the corner behind the old sofa. Finally he felt as if he could approach the world without spewing his guts on the carpet – not that he minded doing that. It wasn't his place after all.

"What happened in here, for fuck's sake?"

Donny shook his head. "Don't ask me. I heard something rattle over by the door and there was a puff of smoke – then I was out cold. I woke up just before you did."

Rico looked over at Knoff and Eric. "Well, did you guys have our backs or what the fuck happened. And where is the girl?"

"She was gone when we got back in here."

"That's impossible! She was obviously taken and you guys are going to sit there and tell me you saw or heard nothing?" Rico was really getting the ire up now as his cohort looked like whipped sheep. He couldn't stand that look and really didn't want to think that he had been knocked out and helpless. "How long was I out?"

Knoff answered. "About twelve hours."

"And you guys just sat here and let me sleep? Didn't load me into the truck or anything? Didn't have the common sense to know that whoever knocked me out would surely come back and finish the job. Why didn't they?"

He looked around the room and no one had an answer. Rico felt his blood pressure ratchet up another couple notches. "You fucking morons are totally useless. I want some answers and all I get is blank stares."

"Well, we didn't see anything, ain't that right Knoff?"

Rico glared at Eric. "When I want to hear something from you I'll rattle my zipper. You morons were supposed to dig a grave so we could dump the chick's body. Instead I wake up to find that she is gone and you guys are sitting around. Not even getting us out of here. You just don't think!"

He walked over and opened the door. Immediately about a dozen red dots sprang up on his chest. His heart rate increased exponentially as he sprang to the side and slammed the door. His first thought was to dive for the floor and scramble out of the way.

A loud speaker outside confirmed what he already knew. This is the FBI. Come out with your hands over your heads and no one will get hurt. You have two minutes before we open fire with tear gas and flush you out. I repeat – come out with your hands over your heads."

Knoff had already opened the trapdoor that allowed egress to the back of the cabin and was backing into the hole. Rico quickly followed and let the others fend for themselves. He hurried as fast as he could and heard the trap slam shut as windows broke in the cabin above.

He was out in the open air and fleeing into the woods when the gas canister exploded. The Feds were nowhere to be seen behind the cabin and Rico fled in the direction of a swamp boat he had had the right frame of mind to squirrel away earlier.

The Feds entered the cabin and found no one there. Lead FBI Agent Bernard Grimm looked around the interior and felt his own blood pressure go up until Agent Darnell Tate lifted up the trap door and indicated the hole in the floor.

"Well, they can't have gone far," Grimm concluded. "Break out the dogs and get the chopper in the air. We got fugitives to find and the game is afoot."

He walked back outside and heard the deep throaty noise of the propeller of an airboat. "Cancel the dogs and get that chopper in the air immediately!" He looked in the direction of the bayou and then raced to his car. His crew piled in as he scattered gravel in an attempt to make it to the overpass the boat would have to travel under.

Only minutes later they all piled out and stood upon the over pass looking upstream out over the bayou. The sound seemed to be steadily coming toward them and they leveled their weapons in preparation for taking a shot.

The air boat appeared but no passengers. It passed under the bridge and Agent Grimm had to call for the dogs again. They must have gotten off somewhere back there in the swamp. I don't need to tell you guys your jobs are riding on this case. We have to find the bastards!"

Meanwhile the boat kept on going out toward open water – with a little help now from someone's hand on the rudder from underneath the water. The Feds ignored it and went back to their vehicles to get the dogs involved in the manhunt.

Finally the boat ran up on a small grass knoll and drove the nose in the air. Knoff reached up and turned the switch. One of the agents noted where it had gone to ground just in case they needed to check it out later. Rico and his crew moved around to the other side of the knoll and covered themselves over with grass so the chopper that was coming in wouldn't spot them from the air.

"Well boys, we caught a break. Now let's make it good and escape these bozos."

26 LEAVING THE AREA

Rico and crew pulled into Pidgeon Forge and immediately checked out the night life. It was abundant and Rico was having a hard time which variety to sample first. He finally decided on a blonde who was getting in her BMW.

"That bitch will do me a couple times before she leaves this world!" he chortled as he punched Knoff's shoulder from the back seat. "Don't follow too closely. No need to spook her and I can work up an appetite for her as we cruise."

Knoff nodded and followed instructions. They soon turned off the main road into a gated community. Rico instructed Eric in how to get over the wall and follow her to her apartment. They waited impatiently as he performed his duty. He finally jumped down from the wall beside the gate and swiped an id card that opened the gate for them.

"She is in Building 3, Apartment 18. It's upstairs and there are cameras on both ends of the buildings. Not sure if they're working because I couldn't detect any auto movement in any of them. Maybe just static with wide angle lens."

"Good job. Now we wait a little while to let her get comfortable then we will go up and make her day. Hell, I'll make her bloody millennium! I am feeling very horny after that swim. I'll bet those FBI boys are still trying to figure out which way we went. Poor dogs won't find anything to sniff but I will. Come on boys – she's had enough alone time."

Rico donned a jacket and hat that made him appear to be a local policeman. He liked to keep an assortment of uniform items in the truck just for occasions like this. He boldly marched up the stairs and rang her door bell.

Inside the apartment Ursalla had just taken off her work clothes and had poured herself a wind-down drink of pink Chablis. She was standing in her undies when Rico hit the buzzer. She frowned because she wasn't expecting anyone. She reached into the drawer of her door-side table and retrieved her gun. She slipped a chamois over her shoulders and cracked the door. It was still on the chain. She felt safe.

"Can I help you?" She saw the badge and hat. She relaxed a bit but still didn't open the door more than a crack.

"Yes, ma'am. We are investigating a robbery that occurred today at your neighbor in C16 and are conducting a canvas of their neighbors to determine if anyone saw something out of the ordinary. Have you been at home all day?"

"No, officer. I work during the day and just got home. So I can't add anything. Is Mrs. Jenkins alright?"

Rico kept a serious look on his face in spite of gaining some information that might prove to be valuable. "No, Miss. She had to be taken to a local trauma ward because of them beating her up. She told our inspector that she didn't have anything valuable and they didn't believe her."

"I'll have to go see her. Where did they take her?"

At that moment Knoff kicked the door and busted the chain. Ursalla was thrust off her feet by the impact of the door and crashed back against her couch – to tumble on the floor. She was fortunate that she held onto her gun and had the frame of mind to put a bullet into the stomach of the big guy who towered over her. Rico disappeared when he realized she was loaded.

Ursalla's bullet had caused Knoff to stumble backwards and he went over the balcony. As she slammed the door she heard the thud as his body hit the ground. She didn't realize it but he got up and stumbled toward the truck – which was pulling away.

He grabbed hold of the tailgate and pulled himself into the bed of the truck as Rico shoved the gas to the floor in an attempt to get out of the community. Knoff didn't think Rico even knew he was in the bed of the truck. It really didn't matter much because he was involved in trying to staunch the bleeding. The bitch had gotten him good but he didn't think he would die from it.

Rico broke the gate and the grill on Knoff's truck as he exited the scene. He could already hear sirens. The bitch had lost no time in dialing 9-1-1. He turned left onto a major highway and noted the sign said it was southbound. He was going back into his local haunts by the time the sun arose and he recognized landmarks.

He pulled back into the yard of the cabin at D'lberville Bayou and turned off the engine. "Is it really good sense to come back here?" Eric asked.

Rico snarled something obscene and started toward the cabin. Donnie Brooks yelled at him that Knoff was in the bed of the truck and had a belly wound. Rico returned to the truck and looked on as the others administered to Knoff. The big man was passed out and there was a lot of blood in the truck.

"We have to get him to a hospital," stated Donny.

"No hospitals," Rico stated flatly as he turned away from the truck. "We ain't going to jail because he can't hold his water. Besides, Knoff is too mean to die. Just bring him into the house and make him comfortable."

Donny slammed the tailgate shut and headed for the driver's seat when Rico pulled out his gun and shoved it toward him. "What the fuck do you think you're doing?"

Donny stood his ground. "Knoff needs a doctor and I'm going to take him to get one. He'll die if we don't get him some blood. You can't be so calloused as to not know that."

"Listen to me worm. I don't really give a shit if any of you guys live or die. You aren't going anywhere and that's a fact. I will put a bullet in your brain if you so much as touch those keys. Now toss them over to me. I call the shots here."

Donnie backed down with the gun in his face and helped Eric as they got Knoff out of the truck and into the cabin. The big man was flushed and sweating profusely. "We have to get some clean bandages if he stands a chance of making it," he told the other man.

Rico was beside himself the rest of the day and well into the night. "First you guys go and lose that girl I was fucking and now Knoff goes and gets himself shot up by the girl I wanted to fuck. How much more incompetence do I have to put up with? Jesus! You guys are a weight around my neck. I should just deep six the lot of you and leave the country on my own."

Eric pulled his gun and held it at the ready as Donnie did the same. Rico calmed down after that but there was an uneasy truce between the members the rest of the night.

27 THE FBI GOES NORTH

Bernard Grim, the lead FBI agent was under fire from his boss in Washington and in no mood to mince words as his team filed into their ready room.

"Boys, we got ourselves what is called a shit sandwich. Big bosses back in Washington want this thing closed and settled within 48 hours. And us with no clue as to where these clowns are right now."

Agent Samuel Tate held his hand up. "I wouldn't say that is entirely true, Boss. We just got word that there was an attempted rape and shooting up in Tennessee. Pidgeon Forge to be exact. It sounds like our boys moved their operations north after we flushed them out."

He handed over a copy of the front page of the Pidgeon Forge Gazette and Agent Grimm read it furiously. His eyes caught all the clues that the other agent had marked with yellow highlighter.

He didn't waste much time in making his decision. "We are going to Tennessee boys. Get your stuff loaded and let's hit the road before the clues go cold on this one. They're probably laid up somewhere if their guy lost as much blood as they say he did. Let's go."

Tate smiled. "Our stuff is already in the SUV, Boss. You're backing up if you're waiting on us."

Grimm knew how good his boys were and had a malicious grin on his broad face as he followed them out of the room. There was no way the rapist was going slip away from them again. He was ready to stake his thirty-two years as an FBI agent on that.

Every mile was torture as the agents wanted to arrive a lot sooner than the speed limit would allow. They got pulled over twice and had to show their badges. Those incidents did little to make their angst any less. But they finally arrived and the sun was going down as they pulled into town.

Their approach was to stop in at the local police station where they were told the victim had gone to stay with her parents in Centerville. Another five hours on the road.

Lead Agent Grimm left instructions for the local Sheriff to contact the witness and tell her the FBI was coming to her. She had orders to stay where she was.

Grimm read all the evidence the local law had on the case as they made their way at ninety-five miles an hour down the western side of Interstate 40.

"They didn't get a whole lot," he said from the front passenger seat. Seems the investigator didn't even arrive until about twenty minutes after the perps left the scene. They interviewed the girl and she didn't give them much. Just something about a local leo going around the community asking some questions about a break-in that happened earlier in the day."

Agent Bernard Evans was driving. He had to keep his attention on the road with the speed he was driving. Nevertheless he asked the question on all their minds. "What about hospitals? Surely they would have taken a stomach wound into one of the local hospitals. Wouldn't they?"

Grimm was shaking his head. "All the local places were checked within six hours of the incident. Nothing. Either the guy died of his wounds or the gunshot wasn't as bad as they tried to make out. But you guys saw the amount of blood on the sidewalk and one of her comments was that he fell over the balcony. I think we're looking for a body by this point. How soon until we arrive?"

Evans looked at his GPS unit. "About two hours. We should get to Centerville about nine and then her father's place is about another forty-five minutes from there."

Grimm settled into his seat and determined to mentally work through the case. His stare out the window reminded his team that they needed to let him stew on things. It was useless to interrupt him when he got in one of his black moods.

It lightened somewhat when they pulled into the yard at the farm. Agent Grimm knew it was late but knocked on the door anyway and stepped back as the porch light flickered on.

Ursulla's father opened the door with a shotgun in the crook of his arm. Agent Grimm introduced himself and his crew and asked to come in. Mr. French stood aside and rested the gun in a corner beside the door.

"We were called by the Sheriff over in Pidgeon Forge about keeping Ursulla here but she ain't going anywhere and we didn't expect you until the morning. But come on in and have a seat. My wife has a pot of coffee going. You fellers are welcome to it."

He led the way into the living room and a few minutes later Ursulla joined them. Her father did the introductions and Agent Grimm got right to the point.

"Is the police report correct in stating you only saw one of the men who tried to attack you?"

Ursulla nodded vigorously. "Yes, sir. I got slammed to the floor when the door was busted in by the guy I shot. I did get a glimpse of another guy who was wearing a ball cap with a police emblem on it."

"Did you get a look at his face?"

"No, sir. His cap was pulled down over his eyes and he seemed to be looking down – like he knew there was a security camera above the door. Daddy insisted on installing that."

"And that has helped a lot. Thanks to you, Mr. French, we have our first real look at a man who has terrorized the entire Gulf coast for the last month or so. We were able to get his height and build from the tape but couldn't get any facial features. We did get a lot of good footage on the guy you shot. Unfortunately we think he might have died from his wound."

He stopped as he noticed the big tears streaming down her face. She choked back a sob. "I didn't want to kill anyone," she stated between sobs. "He really gave me no choice. He was there in the door towering over me one moment and grabbing his stomach the next. I didn't want to hurt him bad – just wanted him to get out of my apartment and leave me alone."

Agent Grimm sat back in his chair and waited for her to regain her composure. Finally she separated herself from her father's shoulder and looked at Agent Grimm.

"Why me? I don't remember ever seeing them before in my life. I'm a good girl. I go to work and come home and go to church on Sunday. I don't party and haven't a clue why they wanted to do something like that to me."

"They are criminals. Rapists and murderers. There are half a dozen families who have already been touched by their crimes and you were just a random victim chosen because the leader thought he liked the way you looked. Don't waste time worrying about them. We are going to catch them and they will be punished for their crimes. The FBI always get their man – especially when members of the public help us the way you have. We owe you a debt for what you have done."

Ursulla smiled slightly and sat a little taller beside her father. Mr. French looked at his pocket watch and remarked on the time. "You fellers are welcome to come back in the morning. We need to get us a good night's sleep."

Agent Grimm nodded and stood up. "I think we got what we came for. We might need to contact you later but thanks for letting us in your home and giving us what you have."

They sat in the car waiting for Grimm to decide what to do. Tate finally got his attention. "Where to now, Boss?"

Grimm shook his head. "I guess we really have to backtrack to Pidgeon Forge and check all the hospitals and vets. Anyone who could have provided medical treatment to the man. Who feels like they're competent to drive?"

All of them felt whacked out but Tate decided he could drive for a while and they started back to the scene of the crime.

28 HAVING A SOLID LEAD

Agent Tate shouted with glee. His computer search had turned up their first lead in days. "They found the body of the guy Ms. French shot. He was dumped in the bayou down near that place where we first jumped the guys. Someone tell Grimm we got em!"

Lead Agent Grimm showed up about five minutes later with sleep still in his eyes. The team had been pulling twenty hour days trying to get a lock on the criminals. "Are you certain it is him?"

"Yes, sir. The Biloxi police matched the bullet to the girl's gun already. The report says someone had been trying to dig it out of him with no success. They identified him as Walter Riley aka Knoff. Only address was a cabin out at D'Iberville Bayou. Isn't that where we jumped them before? Talk about the fox going back to where he is familiar."

Grimm lowered himself onto a stool and read the police report. The body had been dumped in the water about half a mile from the old cabin. 'Not too imaginative,' was his first thought.

"Well, we know why we didn't find him up here. Get the guys and pack for the trip back to Biloxi. I want to be there before it gets light in the morning. You got fifteen minutes and we roll."

Agent Tate jumped up and went to inform his fellow agents that they had their marching orders. They jumped at the task of moving out – boredom was beginning to set in.

They were glad to get out of the Pidgeon Forge area. Things were expensive and the only night life tended to shy away from Federal men. Just something about the dress and demeanor turned off most of the locals.

Tate drove all the way back to Biloxi and arranged for their hotel accommodations. At precisely eight o'clock after the next dawn they had their briefing and planning session for the day's recce mission.

"We want no mistakes this time. We go in silently and see if they are still holed up and then beat it back here to get the big boys back in D.C. to make the most of the opportunity. Tate, you will go in through that access road we saw the first time. If they get wind of our presence they will probably try to get past you."

"Deadly force?" Bernard Evans inquired.

"Only if necessary. The big guys want these guys alive so they can have a big public trial. They want the good people of the Gulf Coast to get their money's worth. Personally, I've about had my fill of all the running around we've done on this case. I'm ready to go home and squeeze the wife and kids."

"Same here, Boss. We'll get them this time."

Grimm looked at his agents and realized they were about a haggard looking lot. All of them needed some rest and relaxation. He felt empty inside and couldn't get enthused about the prospects of bring the perps to justice.

He looked at his watch. "Be ready to move out in ten. I got to get something for my stomach on the way."

An hour later they separated and closed the noose on the cabin. There was a wisp of smoke coming from the chimney so they felt safe in assuming their quarry was still in the cabin. They waited the proscribed fifteen minutes on site and then joined back at the SUV.

Grimm looked at his crew under the direct sunlight and made a decision.

"We are all too tired to try to take these guys without having some serious backup. Davenport just sent me a message saying he will have a fresh team here within six hours and be ready to move in for the capture in nine hours. In the meantime we are to stand down and get some rest. Let's go back to the hotel."

Six hours of sleep produced a miracle in his team's outlook on life, liberty and the pursuit of criminals. Agent Tate went to the Air Force base and picked up their relief.

An hour later Lead Agent Grimm had done his pass-down brief and they were on a plane for New York to brief some of the brass on the case as they understood it. Their relief took over and proceeded to make the arrests.

29 THE FEDS CLOSE IN

Sometimes the process of achieving above and beyond the call of duty sneaks up on you in tragic ways. Special Agent Farnsworth wasn't inclined to find that out – but he did.

Team 1 had been ordered back to headquarters for debriefing even though they were the ones who knew the lay of the land and had experience dealing with the perpetrators. Team 2 moved in and proceeded to establish their sphere of operations.

Nathan Farnsworth dispatched Benny Phelps and Renee Broadrick because they were the oldest and youngest on his team. Benny was an experienced veteran of eighteen years – seasoned and able to think accurately in hot situations demanding the utmost of brainpower. Renee was a rookie – not even finished with her training but related to someone in high places. They were put together so one would learn how not to fuck it up.

They walked in from the road where they had parked their SUV. Benny had made sure that Renee had enough gear to keep her feet nailed to the ground – so their movement was slower than normal as she assimilated the actions involved in setting up a stakeout. After about half a mile they inserted themselves into a tall grove of acacia and palm trees and prepared to wait.

They peeped through the tall grass at the front of the cabin just as one of the men inside stepped out onto the porch and had a quick look around. He quickly went back inside and Benny settled down to wait with Renee by his side.

Benny parted the grass a few minutes later and made observations. "Didn't Farnsworth say they only had one truck – a beat up Ford?"

Renee looked at her notes. "Yes. It's that old blue-ish gray thing parked around the side of the house."

"Good observations. Explain all those other trucks and cars that are parked out in the yard. Who do you suppose owns them?"

Renee looked through the grass he was holding aside and counted six vehicles parked in the yard. "You want me to make their license plates?"

"Only the ones you can see from here. We don't want to endanger the job by letting the ones inside know we're here."

He continued observing as she got out her iPad and began entering plate numbers. After a few moments she had information sheets back on three of them.

"Harvey Banks, Michael Taylor and Chris Taylor. All of them have outstanding warrants for their arrest. Mostly petty stuff but Harvey Banks has a disorderly firearms charge. Says he might be armed and dangerous."

Benny looked back at where she sat on the grass. "You'll find they're all armed and dangerous. Never make the mistake of thinking they aren't. Those are the ones that will get you dead."

"I understand that. But what are all these guys doing here? You think he went out and added some men to his gang after that last guy died?"

"What was the name of that last guy? You have to know these things by heart before we release you into the field."

Renee frowned and tried to remember. It almost flashed into her memory but was gone. "His alias was Knoff. I can't remember his name but it will come to me. Just give me a moment."

"You may not have a moment if Farnsworth is asking."

Farnsworth interrupted their education process requesting an update on their position. Benny related all they had found out so far and was told to sit tight.

Meanwhile the other members of the team were making ready to surround the cabin. Benny noticed them as they melted out of the forest and took up positions. He had a bad feeling about the operation at that point and was about to call Farnsworth again when an underground hatch not ten feet in front of them opened up and they began taking automatic fire.

Benny glanced back as he flung himself to one side. A bullet had just passed through Renee's temple and the light went out of her eyes as she was shoved to the ground by the bullet's velocity. His heart broke as he scrambled out of the line of fire.

A bullet ricocheted off a tree and smote him in his right calf muscle. He doubled up in pain and had to use his forearms to crawl away from their hiding place. The fact they had been made didn't escape his cognizance as he struggled to make it out of the area of the fire fight. He realized he hadn't got off a shot and he had lost a comrade.

30 AND BLOW THE CASE

FBI Special Agent Farnsworth was surprised as a hillock sprung up and a hail of bullets raked the forest. He was lucky to be behind an old cypress tree but the soft wood didn't stop the bullets – just slowed them down somewhat. He watched his comms specialist, Daniel Smith as he took a volley that stitched him up the front from his groin to his chin.

Agent Smith was flung back like a rag doll by the impact of the volley and lay still. It was then that Farnsworth realized he had been hit. His right arm was useless and a cop killer had penetrated the left side of his vest. He was losing blood fast as he dove for cover.

Earl Benson stepped up out of his tunnel entrance and checked his efficiency. Both agents were down and he could see arms in the air from Eric and Donny. They were celebrating their own kills. Earl turned around and walked back to his fox hole where he lowered the trap door. He closed it and went across the long side of the yard to see the other agents that were down. None of them moved.

He sauntered back into the cabin and approached Rico. "They have all met their maker. Now what?"

Rico looked up with a sour countenance. "Since I was out voted we are now responsible for the killing of Federals. The FBI doesn't forget when one of their own gets laid low. How many did we take out today – five, six?"

"We took down six and can do it again. The next group won't know what hit them. Those cop killers work well."

Earl went over to the small fridge and proceeded to fix himself a sandwich. "You need to get over yourself. Knoff was just in the wrong place at the wrong time. Any of us can take a bullet and it was his time to go. Scratch and get over it before we do something that will get us all killed."

"I'm afraid we already have," Rico countered as he walked out the door and tried to get some cool air into his lungs. He felt like he was going to explode and it wasn't because of Knoff. Rico just wanted to get laid – in the worst way. His balls were aching and he didn't see a woman anywhere.

Rico shrugged and went back inside. He grabbed the keys from where they lay on the table and stomped back out of the room.

"Where the hell are you going?" Earl inquired.

"Out! Just out. I gotta get laid." The trucks tires kicked up gravel when he peeled out of the parking lot. Earl followed his progress all the way to the main road and then turned to the others to remark, "Now boys, you know some poor soul is going to die before he gets back. Maybe two or three. I've never seen him in a mood as black as that."

"You think he's got a death wish, don't you?" Donny said from the sofa. He put down his iPhone and looked around the room. It was obvious to him that he might have said the wrong thing.

Earl lost no time in setting him straight. He was in Donny's face before the others could blink. "Listen here fool! I been with that man for over a dozen years and I ain't never seen him like this before. We have to stick together now or all of us are going to die. Just don't say nothing to his face. He whack you for sure."

"Hey, man. I didn't mean nothing by it. It's his business but I just don't want to see him do something that will get us caught."

"He won't. Rico knows how to take the back alleys."

Eric was standing at the door listening to the conversation. "I say we get our things and get out of here while he's gone. That's what I would do."

Earl rounded on him. "That's what you would do, huh?"

"Yes. We need to get out of here before someone comes in here looking for them FBI men. And don't tell me to take the bodies and feed them to the crocs. I'm tired of doing all the dirty work."

Earl pulled his gun from the back of his jeans and took a couple steps toward the door. "Listen here, fool. You will do the jobs you're assigned. I'm in charge while Rico is gone and I say we take care of the bodies. We don't need nothing left here that can point back to us. And we will be moving out – just as soon as Rico gets back."

The other guys looked at Earl and knew he meant business. Donny got up off the couch and patted Earl on the shoulder as he walked by. Earl shrugged him off and he continued out the door – along with Eric. They had a job to do.

Stanley Volgamore drove up while the guys were out doing their task. He always got right to the point.

"I hear you boys had a run in with the law."

"Where did you hear that?"

"Ran into Rico about a hour ago. He took two of my girls and split. Reckon he's going to give them back?"

"Probably not," Earl said with a shrug. "Doesn't matter. He's just trying to get back in the groove. No use to sweat it."

"Well, I am sweating it. Them girls bring me at least five big bills a night. I want them back in one piece – unharmed or I'm going to the cops myself. There's a big reward posted on you lot. I could use it to relocate. So you get on the phone and tell Rico he better not harm either of them. You got that?"

"Yeah, I got it." Earl raised his arm – a shot rang out and a body slammed backwards into the floor. Stanley had a neat, dark hole leaking blood just inside the doorway. The boys came running up and Earl indicated there was another body for them to dispose of.

"Do him yourself," Donny exclaimed. "I want no more to do with this." He turned to leave when a gas canister exploded between them. None of them knew they hit the floor. They were gathered up to await the return of Rico.

31 CAPTURE, INTERROGATION & TRIAL

Rico was having his way with several young ladies at the moment the gas canister exploded. His semen was dripping from the nether regions of both as he lay back and viewed his work. Both were also bleeding from cuts made to their throats at the moment of their individual orgasms. He considered himself an artist – one dealing in the macabre for sure. But an artist by any means.

"One day the entire world will ascribe glory and honor to me for my consummate work. They will say my name as many times as they now call on their errant savior. I will be famous."

He sat up and remembered he needed to be somewhere. He just couldn't remember where. "I have a time to be somewhere," he stated to the two virgins he had placed side by side. "Why can't I remember? Tell me!"

Rico sat on the edge of the bed and slipped his feet into his shoes while he tried to recall where he was supposed to be going. Slipping a ball cap on his head he left the scene – none the wiser.

He made it back to the cabin and stepped inside the door before he realized that where he was wasn't where he wanted to be. He tried to turn and run back to the truck but someone stopped his progress with their rather large body.

Former FBI Agent Ronald Benoit stepped into his line of sight as Desmond Howard securely fastened Rico's arms to his sides.

"What is this?" he started to protest.

"This is your capture. Soon we will have the interrogation. Then the trial and finally – an execution. Rico Sanchez – you will be shown the same mercy you've shown to all your victims. You will be punished for your crimes against humanity and you will pay in both your blood and your tears."

Benoit swept his right hand around the room. "These are your judges and I will be your executioner. Get to know our faces. That is all you will know of us. We are called the 'Gravediggers' and we take our mission seriously. Any questions so far?"

Rico stood in shock – as did the other members of his gang who were tied to individual support beams around the room. He was having a hard time fathoming the fact that he was caught. That had never been part of his plan.

"Are you FBI?" he asked.

Benoit had turned away from him but now he returned to stand in front of Rico. "No. We are not FBI or any other form of government agency. So, as you will come to see, we are not bound by their rules and regulations. And you have no rights inside this tribunal."

Benoit glanced over at Melinda Howard and she stepped forward. "Rico Sanchez. You are hereby under the jurisdiction of the court of law of the Gravediggers. First you will be interrogated. How do you plead?"

"What do you mean? How do I plead? You have no call to be thinking you can treat me like this! I am not a criminal to be bound up like some animal. I demand you let me go."

Sammy Blackman stepped forward as the prosecuting attorney and identified himself as such. "My learned defense attorney will be Mr. Howard over there. He will represent you during the trial. Now be so kind as to answer the judge. Are you guilty or not?"

"Of what? You haven't even read the charges yet!" Rico began to struggle in his restraints – to no avail.

Melinda cleared her throat. "Yes. Well, I have a list of the charges right here." She lifted a sheet of paper and began to read from it.

"Rico Sanchez, you stand here accused of nine counts or murder. Add roughly a dozen counts of kidnapping, rape, gang rape and sodomy. Your crimes against society include the gunning down of roughly seven to eight law enforcement officers and the grisly disposal of their bodies and we can paint a picture of so much degradation that would make normal people shake in terror to be around you. What is your plea?"

"Now listen. I didn't kill them FBI agents. That was all Earl's doings. And you have no evidence to try to pin anything but consensual sex on me. I didn't kill anyone. And I didn't do any raping. The girls like me."

"Your protest are noted. Mr. Benoit, you have evidence to the contrary, I believe?"

Benoit stepped forward again and held up his cell phone. He hit playback and everyone heard the distressed voice of Knoff – relating how he assisted Rico in not only securing the young ladies in question, but participated in the rapes and witnessed the murder of the individuals girls.

His testimony was damning and Rico's shoulders slumped as his old friend listed the litany of girls and atrocities.

Melinda asked a quiet question. "Now how do you plead? Are you the man detailed in that testimony?"

"Knoff was my friend and would never turn on me like that."

"But he did. You let him die. And that was his deathbed version of what you did to all those girls. He was even happy at the end to get it all off his chest. Made him die with a smile on his big face." Benoit turned back to Rico and stabbed him in the chest with his finger.

"Do you have any idea why we are here?

Rico shook his head – desperate to find some place to hide.

None was available and his legs quaked as he realized he might not be able to get out of this situation. His pants were damp in front as he started to lose control of his nervous system. His bladder was doing its best to betray him – just like his friends.

Melinda's gaze took in the rest of the room and came to rest on Rico's cronies. "You guys have anything to say?"

Donnie was the first to crack under her glare. "It was Rico. He wouldn't let us take Knoff to a hospital and he's the one who got Knoff shot in the first place. It's justice that he reached out from the grave to finger the bastard. Things always had to be done his way. I shouldn't never have taken up with him. Only did it because of Knoff."

Melinda asked after a moment, "Did you participate in the rapes?"

Donny stammered. "Only one. And she really liked the way I was gentle with her. Hell, anyone would be gentle after Knoff did them. He was hung like a horse."

"Guilty." She turned to Earl.

"What was your involvement?"

Earl lowered his head. With belligerence he let it be known he didn't consider their questioning to be legal or fair.

"I'll get no justice from you. This kangaroo court is a farce! I'll not be judged by you."

"Guilty."

Eric knew he was next. "I didn't rape anyone. Nor did I witness the murders of them girls. I did go along with Earl and Rico regarding the FBI. They were sneaking up on us and we were determined not to be taken in."

Desmond Howard spoke for the first time. "Maybe you should have let them take you in. That way you would have spent years in the courts of the land, fed by taxpayers and eventually given free room and board for the rest of your lives."

He turned to the jurors. "My clients should have thought of that. They didn't and here they stand before a court of justice. They could throw themselves on the mercy of the court."

Rico exploded. "Where the hell is this court of justice? You're just another gang of thugs. There ain't no justice here and you know it. I demand to see a real lawyer."

Desmond stepped in front of him and held out a certificate that read he could practice law in the state of Mississippi. "You see? We are prepared for every eventuality."

Rico remained furious but it mattered little to members of the court. None were in the least fazed by his continuing theatrics. All had come to the same conclusion – it is a terror to fall under the auspices of the Gravediggers.

32 ADMISSION OF GUILT

Rico quailed and lost his water. It ran freely down the front of his pants as he suddenly realized he wasn't going to be extricated from his situation. Nothing short of a miracle was going to save him now. And miracles seemed far away as Desmond stepped back and faced the judge.

"Madam judge, we have a miscreant who would like to confess his sins."

"This isn't a place where clergy robes are worn," she remarked. "Your client does realize he has fallen victim to those who care less whether he lives or dies?"

"Yes, Ma'am. I think he finally does. Or at least he partially knows the extent of his fall from grace. I move that we give the accused an opportunity to address the court in their defense."

"Permission granted." Melinda looked directly at Rico and he couldn't hold her eyes. He tried looking anywhere but where he really should have.

"Well, the court is ready, Mr. Sanchez. What do you have to say for yourself regarding the charges read against you?"

Rico tried to clear his throat but found his mouth had no saliva. He struggled against his bonds and again tried not to raise his eyes to meet hers.

"Your honor, I throw myself on the mercy of the court."

"You have not that right," she stated flatly. "When you took it on yourself to rape and murder – you lost the rights afforded to most criminals in our society. And when you killed those FBI agents you really sealed your fate. You should have gone quietly with them. You would be in prison but you would also be safe."

Rico blanched and his breath wouldn't come fast enough for him to clear his head. He tried to find something else to say but no cogent thoughts would invade his brain. He stood there with his head bowed.

"We are waiting, Mr. Sanchez. The members of this tribunal are really interested in the forces that drove you to take the lives of so many innocent young girls."

Rico raised his head. "I don't have to provide you with anything. My reasons were my own and you are not my judge."

Melinda looked around the room. "You've said that before. I think you are good at ducking the real issues. But we shall see what kind of answers you get after we sequester you for a while. Bailiff, take him away and put him in the hotbox. Make sure he has water. I don't want him dying on us. Now as for the rest of Rico's crew."

Clint Black roughly grabbed Rico's left arm and jerked him toward the door. Rico screamed and got a backhand for his efforts. Those still in the room turned their eyes to the other guys on trial. The charges were again read and confessions readily poured from lips eager to get their sins put behind them.

The tribunal took a lunch break and it was after two o'clock before Rico was brought back into the courtroom. His head had been put inside a nasty smelling black bag. Clint removed it from his head and Rico tried to breathe deeply. He was shoved roughly into the prisoner's box that had been improvised from pieces of broken furniture.

"Now, Mr. Sanchez. I think we have business to conclude. We have another gig to get on to when this trial is concluded. Now be a good boy and tell the court what we want to know."

Rico again tried to look anywhere but in her direction. His eyes caught on Benoit who was standing on one corner. He was working on a wicked looking sickle – put an edge on a once rusty blade. The implement had been hanging over on one wall since they had arrived. Benoit fingered the blade as if judging whether it was going to be sharp enough. He shook his head and moved over behind Earl.

Earl collapsed onto his knees as Benoit grabbed a hank of his hair. His eyes teared up as he realized it was his time. Benoit placed the sickle in front of Earl's throat and pulled it back and sideways. With difficulty Earl's throat opened up and he belched blood up through the opening. Benoit continued to hold his head erect and Earl began to choke.

Rico lost his determination at that point. He tried to close his eyes but Clint hit him in the kidneys and he couldn't decide which stimuli to respond to. Earl was still struggling. The cut wasn't enough to kill him outright. The look on his face was enough to terrify anyone. Rico again lost his water.

He looked at Melinda as Earl finally lost most of his hold on life. Benoit stepped forward and placed the blade again in front of Earl's throat. He jerked back hard and a scream issued from the man as his head was severed from his body. The body toppled forward and Benoit held up the head. Rico screamed.

When he could finally maintain a little control of himself Rico addressed the court again. "I admit I may have taken liberties that I probably shouldn't have. Please just put a bullet in my brain. I really don't want to go the same way."

"What same way?" asked Melinda.

"I don't want him to use that dull sickle on me. Please, don't do it!"

"Then confess what you've done."

"Okay. I confess. I raped and killed all those girls. That's the only way I could get off. Are you satisfied now?"

"Exactly."

33 BRADLEY JUSTICE EXPLAINED

Melinda called for a brief recess as the Gravediggers propped Earl's body in the corner and hoisted it on a rope toward the low roof. Not a movement was lost on Rico or the rest of the gang. They were made to understand they would end their lives in the same manner.

"I guess we've seen enough," she said as she banged an old tin cup on the battered desk to call the trial back into session.

"Mr. Rico Sanchez. Your attention please. We still have some business to dispense with before we carry out the dispositions of this court."

Rico couldn't quite keep his knees from quaking. At least he didn't have anything in his bladder so he couldn't embarrass himself in front of everyone again.

"What kind of business?"

"I'm glad you asked. You see, you can be as surly as you want to but the final dictates have already been handed down by the lady who hired us."

"Then you are just vigilantes for hire. Is that it?"

"In so many terms. We were wrapping up a job in Montana when a lady called us from Biloxi to see if we wanted to take this job of bringing the murderer of her grandchild to justice."

Rico swallowed hard as the meaning of justice settled in. He wasn't going to get out of this one. These folks had already been paid to string him up. His head ached as he considered what had happened to him. He had totally been set up.

Melinda continued and her words at first were unintelligible as Rico tried to concentrate but found it difficult. She paused to allow him to catch up.

"Pay attention, Mr. Sanchez. I don't like repeating myself."

"Mrs. Margaret Bradley employed us to find you. She did not want us to turn you over to the authorities. The FBI was to have no access to you.

You were to be captured and placed on trial. The charges, specifically that of the torture, rape and murder of her dear grand-daughter, Charlotte, were to be read to you and you are to be removed from this mortal coil in the most lingering, damaging and painful manner that can be devised.

Mr. Sanchez, you will now be stripped of your name and identity. You will henceforth no longer be called by the Christian name you so defiled but shithead. You will be addressed as the feral animal that you are. You will be given no leniency. Nor will anyone from henceforth offer you solace. Do you understand these arrangements?"

Rico could only quake as the enormity of his situation settled into his brain. He was lost – not only lost but completely cut off from all humanity.

Mrs. Bradley wanted us to notify her only after you are dead. We have and will continue to tape this trial and execution. You have been found guilty of crimes against humanity. You will pay for your atrocities against those whose lives you so willingly took from them. But you will die especially for the heinous manner in which you raped and murdered Charlotte Bradley. It is only with regret that we cannot execute you for each individual's life."

Melinda banged the tin cup against the battered desk and pronounced the verdict.

"Death. What say you, members of the tribunal?"

Each Gravedigger in turn pronounced their verdict – Death.

"So have you been judged and so shall it be carried out. You have one day to focus upon your transgressions. Then the verdict will be carried out."

Rico slumped to his knees in abject terror. The thought flashed through his mind that the stay of 24 hours was more than he could bear. Maybe he could find a way to end his life before they had a chance.

That did not avail. He was bound and lifted high to dangle above the ground. He couldn't move – no way could he take his own life.

34 WRAPPING UP THE SCENE

Rico was terrified out of his wits. Eight verdicts of guilty had been given and Benoit approached with that wicked looking dull sickle. A severe ache in his throat caused Rico to gag as Benoit stood behind him and grabbed his hair.

Benoit took his time – which infuriated Rico. "Get it over with," he screamed and at the same time defecated his pants. If he could have felt shame at that point he was certain he would have but they were past that now.

Benoit leaned forward. "You can wait just a little longer, now can't you? We have to change the angle of the camera or so I'm told. Wouldn't want to get in the swing of things and find out things aren't quite right. After all, you are the star of the show."

He laughed and pulled Rico's head taut. The sickle was placed in front of Rico's throat but wasn't drawn across – it just lay on the skin. Rico's body shook involuntarily.

"Would the shithead like to say anything before the sentence is carried out?" Melinda asked.

Rico couldn't think straight. Terror had set in. In all his days he had never guessed he would end up like this. Civilized people didn't do these things to other people – no matter what they had done. It just wasn't done. A lengthy trial, with judge, jury and appeals – that was normal in modern society. Spending many years on the taxpayers dime – but not this!

It suddenly hit him that he might be feeling the same thing his victims had felt at the moment he stuck his switchblade in their throats. Maybe they too had thought he should have let them go. Maybe he could have been more lenient with his victims and not taken so much pleasure in watching them die.

He screamed and lost his mind. At that moment the sickle was drawn across his throat. It bit deep and was as dull as Rico had imagined. The pain was off the scale as blood gurgled from the wound. Rico's eyes went dim as his breath would no longer support his lungs. He drowned in his own fluids and toppled forward to lay face down on a dirty wooden floor.

Benoit reached down and removed the head – to hold it up for the camera. Rico Sanchez would never kidnap, rape and kill any other innocent women. His escapades were finished.

35 EXITING THE GULF COAST

Ronald Benoit had delivered the tape to Margaret Bradley. The 89 year old southern lady thanked him and paid for the team's services. He took his leave from her and a load seemed to lift from his shoulders.

The day was bright with sunshine as he drove down to the beachfront to meet his team. They all sat in a gazebo and watched him approach.

"Was she satisfied with the tape?" Desmond Howard asked from his spot in the back of the gazebo.

"I don't know," Benoit replied. "She just laid it on the stand beside her bed and thanked me for it."

"She didn't ask if he was dead?" Rosie inquired.

Benoit shook his head as he sat in the only vacant spot and looked at his team. "No, she didn't ask. I'm sure she will view the tape in a day or two. She only asked if there were any way of anyone identifying us on the tape and I told her we all wore masks. She was pleased with that."

Silence lengthened as each of them contemplated what had been done. Benoit finally broke their reverie.

"Listen. We did some things on this job that were a little beyond the pale. I think we all knew that would happen going in to this job. And it did. We were way outside the law, but the job had to be done. We did it according to the wishes of Mrs. Bradley. At the age of 89 she didn't have time to wait for the normal course of justice to take its due course. We did her a favor by handling it as we did. I feel little remorse for it and neither should any of you."

He looked into the eyes of each member of the Gravediggers. There was no indication anywhere that any of them felt they had done a miscarriage to justice.

"Anyway, we are each one million dollars richer. We can do a lot for the cause of justice with that amount. What do you say we mount our bikes and get out of here? Kansas City is calling and I want a nice long vacation before we take on our next case."

They all filed past and within half an hour they had departed the Gulf Coast – heading north – to other adventures.

Characters and Place Names

Team Members (The Grave Diggers)

Ronald Benoit	Team leader
Sammy Blackman	Team Infiltration expert
Rose Morales	Team physical evidence
Desmond Howard	Team scientist
Russell Crowe	Team second in command
Ben Jameson	Team Tracker
Clint Black	Team Tracker
Melinda Howard	Team Hardware expert

Criminals

Rico Jaurez Sanchez	
Knoff (Walter Riley)	
Earl Benson	
Eric Riley	
Donny Brooks	
Mr. Stanley Volgamore	Criminal mastermind/fence

FBI Agents (Team 1)

Bernard Grimm	Lead FBI Agent
Samuel Tate	FBI second in command
Bernard Evans	FBI Investigator
Darnell Tate	FBI Investigator

FBI Agents (Team 2)

Nathan Farnsworth	Lead FBI Agent
Benjamin Phelps	FBI second in command
Daniel Smith	FBI Investigator
Simon Ware	FBI Investigator
Jennifer Daniels	FBI Investigator
Renee Broadrick	FBI Investigator

Local Law Enforcement

Jerome Tackett	Biloxi Sheriff
Morgan Smith	Deputy
Alice Adkinson	Forensics/Coroner
Mervin Smith	Patrolman
Ginger Ling	Patrolwoman
Maggie Bernard	Dispatcher

Victims

Case File #601	Charlotte Bradley	Age: 22
Case File #602	Tina Marie Comer	Age: 26
Case File #604	Mary Alice Daniels	Age: 19
Case File #605	Randi Somers	Age: 20
Case File #712	Jeanie Sherman	Age: 15
Case File #713	Barbie Simmons	Age: 12
	Tommy Beach	Age: 17
	Ursulla French	Age: 23

Client

Mrs. Margaret Bradley	Grandmother of 1st victim

Locals

Jeb Adkins	Bike shop owner
Sammy Adkins	Bike shop manager
Trace Jones	Mechanic
Misha Sherman	Jeanie's mother
Norah Thompson	Flop house owner
Douglas Rose	Grocery store manager
Tommy Beach	Barbie Simmons boy friend
Ginny Brooks	antagonist, friend of Earl Benson

Locations

Highway 49
State Route 10
Biloxi
Gulfport

Pensacola
The Half Shell
The Bonefish Grill
D'lberville Bayou

Gravedigger Bio's

Ronald Benoit   Team leader

5'10", 190 lbs, grey eyes, slightly greying hair, 45 years old
Ex-FBI Team Leader. Benoit resigned after the Pleistocene Pig debacle. His disgust with the bureaucracy was evident following the mission debrief in which he and his team were blamed for most everything that happened. Benoit established an investigative agency called the Ghostriders because everyone rode Harleys and loved their choppers. He also changed the mode of operation from inside the law to outside the system.

Sammy Blackman   Team Infiltration expert

5'9", 210 lbs, brown eyes, brown hair, 36 years old, tattoo on inside of wrists of snake. That is why his nickname is Snake. He is an expert infiltrator and surveillance man and is not afraid of 'stepping outside the law' to get result. A survivor of Afghanistan before joining the FBI. He is also an expert weapons handler and a 9th degree black belt in several martial arts. He is an only child and parents were murdered when he was 14.

Rose Morales   Team physical evidence

5'5", 115 lbs, blonde, blue eyes, 32 years old, 2 bullet wounds from a drive-by shooting when she was a teenager. She is the forensic expert for the team and is not afraid to do whatever it takes to get the job done. She would follow Benoit and the team through hell and gone and has no love for organized crime or law enforcement following the PPG incident.

Desmond Howard   Team scientist

6'2", 220 lbs, African American, brown eyes, bald, 39 years old. Married. No children. Expert with explosives and surveillance devices. Can break into any closed space or vehicle. Has no qualms about going under cover to track the bad guys and no love for the FBI after PPG. He is the 'work-out' expert and has designed a regimen for the entire team.

Russell Crowe   Team second in command

6"0", 200 lbs, Blackfoot Indian/German heritage, brown eyes, black hair, 40 years old. Not married. Prefers to live alone but will accept close ties with team members. Expert tracker who prides himself in never losing a man after he begins to track. He also has no qualms about operating outside the law. He is an expert marksman with several weapons and is also expert in hand to hand combat. He likes to develop surveillance systems and is a handy gadget man.

Ben Jameson   Team Tracker

5'9", 185 lbs, Cherokee/Scottish heritage, brown eyes, black hair, 42 years old. Not married. No family and no ties to anyone except members of the team. Expert tracker – in fact he is probably the best tracker in North America. Has a souped up Hog that he designed himself. Is an expert marksman and knows hand to hand combat tactics.

Clint Black   Team Tracker

Ex-rodeo star. Expert marksman and hand to hand combat expert. Loves horses and all things outdoors. Can survive in the wild on his own. Never married. Only allegiance is to the team. Despises upper management at the FBI and blames them for the team's troubles following PPG. Is an excellent infiltrator and doesn't mind getting his hands dirty.

Melinda Howard   Team Hardware expert

5'6", 110 lbs, African American/Hawaii ancestry, married to Desmond Howard. Loves all things gadgets and can design any tool in minutes from discarded junk. She only talks to and through her husband. Has a phobia about crowds and doesn't perform well in mixed company. She has two martial arts belts and doesn't like being touched. She designs most of the gadgets the team uses to do their job. She can hack into any computer system and has designed a computer based comms system that the team uses that can't be jammed or detected.

ABOUT THE AUTHOR

Tim Conley really began writing at the young age of six when he would recount his daydreams to whoever would listen. His authoritarian father discouraged this and any other action that smelled of books and reading. Tim would sneak into any hidden away corner and escape through the avenue of reading and was known as a loner and dreamer by his classmates, preferring his own company and that of 'made-up characters' to that of friends. Now at age 60, Tim has a huge amount of material to draw from to create his own settings and characters.

Tim is still a loner, living with his wife and lover, Carmela Santos (a teacher from the Philippines). He would like to run a small ranch with a couple horses, some pigs and chickens and enjoys gardening.

Tim is satisfied to live the quiet life of a simple man. He studied writing at the University College at Memphis State University. The fact is he enjoys writing more than all the other things he has accomplished in life. Teaching for inner city schools has provided excitement in his life, but he has configured a quiet place where he can sit at the computer during the evening to recount his 'thoughts of the day...dream.'

Tales From Avalon is not the first and only writing that Tim has done. Tim also has TRANSDEM, INC. and The Curse of Indian Gold that were published by Brandywine Books and PublishAmerica. He is currently working on the fifth book of a space opera named Journey to Mars. He has published Memoirs of a Country boy, Crystal Possession: Vanessa's Story, Crystal Possession: Imagination Island and Dark Moons on Chimera, among others.

Other titles by this author can be found at www.dbponline.net:

Sci-fi category:

Transdem, Inc.,	Omegan Arrival
	Escape into Elsewhere
	Saval's Revenge
	The Ends of the Universe
Crystal Possession:	Vanessa's Story
	Imagination Island
Journey to Mars:	The Awakening
	Blood is Forever
	To Fight the Evil
	The Vampire Underground
	The Denebian Connection

Tales from Avalon
    Avalon, Book 1 – The Avalonian Connection *
    Avalon, Book 2 – Genesis: To Outrun a Nova *
    Avalon, Book 3 – The Toltec Expedition *
    Avalon, Book 4 – The Chen Lao Conspiracy *
    Avalon, Book 5 – The Oludavi Revelation *
    Avalon, Book 6 – 2013: The Melting Pot *
    Avalon, Book 7 – 2023: Life Here After *
A One-Way Trip
Operation Arachnid: On High Alert
Wolfsden X at Sirius IV
gematra
Withdrawn from Man
Moon Base Alpha
Trace
Age of Reason
Cloning – Am I Me?
More Avalonian Tales

Historical Fiction
Escape from Jamestown
The Primitive Shoppe
It Won't be long now
How Did It Happen?
In the Shadow of the Sword

Religious Issues and Comments
What is on the Other Side?
The Documentary Hypothesis
The Epistle of Third Timothy
It Won't be long now

Horror category:
The Curse of Indian Gold
A Tale of Cardiff Glen
Cloning: Am I Me?
The White Chapel Murders: Jill the Ripper
Pleistocene Pig

Fantasy:
Dark Moons on Chimera:
      Birth under a Sign
      The Adventures of Kn'Ross
      The Tribulations of Kn'Rose
      The Triple Thrones of Theuniss

Biography/Poetry category:
Memoirs of a Country boy
Poetic License
Thunder Breaks in on Silence
Short Stories, Essays and Comments
Grandma Conley's Family
The Life and Times of Ruth Yothers
A Poetic Life   Gertrude Bonincontro

How-To category:
Writing 101: For Beginners
How To: Excel
How To: Access
How to Write Fiction
How to Repair Old Computers

Screenplays:
A Screenplay: Immoral Authority
A Screenplay: Joseph & Asseneth

Murder Mystery
Murder by Design (David Paffrath)
A Twisted Fate (David Paffrath)
Tommy knockers (David Paffrath)
Hit Men Don't Make Good Daddies
Til Death do us part

The Margo Bryant Chronicles:
    Caribbean Blue
    Under a Yellow Sea
    The Red Pentagon
    Sinking in Green Triangles
    The Case of Black Death
    The White Chill
    The Forensic Diaries (Destiny Stone)
    EVOL LOVE (Destiny Stone)
    A Day in the Life (Destiny Stone)

Doctoral Theses
British Women Travel Writers   (Alison Day)
Relationship between Demographic Variables and Self-Efficacy in Three On-Line Post Graduate Department Programs   (Gertrude Bonincontro)
Followership in the Tri-States   (Thomas Steinback)

40091103R00080

Made in the USA
Charleston, SC
24 March 2015